FAIRY TALES

EASY STEP-BY-STEP PROJECTS THAT TEACH SCISSOR SKILLS

Written and illustrated by Kim Rankin

Teaching & Learning Company
1204 Buchanan St., P.O. Box 10
Carthage, IL 62321-0010

This book belongs to

____

Cover by Kim Rankin

ISBN No. 1-57310-115-X

Printing No. 98765432

Teaching & Learning Company
1204 Buchanan St., P.O. Box 10
Carthage, IL 62321-0010

TABLE OF CONTENTS

Dear Teacher or Parent,

"I did it myself" is a phrase which can be the foundation for a lifetime of accomplishment and positive self-esteem.

Cut and Create activities can be used by the teacher or parent to develop a variety of important early skills and to provide projects in which children can take pride and succeed.

- Simple patterns and easy, step-by-step directions develop scissor skills and give practice in visual-motor coordination. The scissor rating system in the upper right-hand corner on the first page of each project quickly identifies the easiest projects (✂), moderate (✂✂) and challenging (✂✂✂).
- Materials used are inexpensive and readily available.
- Finished products are fun, colorful and have myriad uses from play items to props; room decorations for walls, bulletin boards or mobiles; learning center manipulatives for counting, sorting, classifying or labeling; gifts or favors for parties or guests; and much more.

The simple and fun activities included in this book will help young learners build a solid base for a variety of skills such as: following directions, observation, discrimination and information processing. Various learning styles are addressed including visual, auditory and tactile.

Your art program, whether structured or serendipitous, can benefit from these simple and sequenced scissor skill activities. Your students will

- develop manual dexterity
- communicate
- learn to control his or her environment by being responsible for tools and materials
- observe
- discriminate (by color, shape, texture)
- sort, order, group and engage in other math processes
- imagine!

We hope you and your students will enjoy these projects. They have been designed to stimulate learning and creativity in a way that is simple and fun. So go cut and create! And have a good time!

Sincerely,

Kim

Kim Rankin

Suggestions for Using Some of the Projects

Different Uses

- Bulletin Boards
- Ceiling Decorations
- Flannel Board Figures
- Greeting Cards (Reduce 30-40%)
- Mobiles
- Paper Bag Puppets
- Party Favors
- Rebus Rhymes
- Refrigerator Magnets (Reduce 25-40%)
- Stick Puppets/Finger Puppets
- Tabletop or Desk Decorations
- Take-Homes for Parents
- Window/Door Decorations
- Portfolio Pieces
- Folders (Reduce 30-50%)

Bulletin Boards

Copy figures and display on bulletin board covered with background paper. (Shown here: figures from the Little Red Hen [pages 45-49] with student chore sign-up.)

Rebus Rhymes

Copy the rhyme.
Use figures for words wherever possible.

Mobiles

Here are two suggestions for making a mobile. One way is to use a sturdy paper plate for the top piece. Punch holes around the outer edge of the plate. Use string or yarn in random lengths to attach the ready-made patterns to the top piece.

Another way is to use sturdy tagboard. Cut a rectangle shape approximately 3" x 32" (8 x 56 cm) and staple the ends together to form a circle. Punch holes around the bottom edge. Use string or yarn in random lengths to attach the ready-made patterns. (Note: You will have to reduce the patterns 40 to 50% so they are not too big for the mobile.)

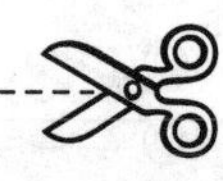

Greeting Cards

Celebrate a holiday or create an occasion. Handmade greeting cards are a surefire hit for parents, grandparents, relatives and friends. And what better way to say "thank you" to a visitor, custodian, principal, helper, etc.

Window/Door Decorations

Attach figures to door or window for a welcome-to-school, parent conference or special occasion display. Add extra pieces, if required. (Shown here: enlarged pigs from pages 33-40.)

Flannel Board Figures

Cut figures from flannel instead of paper, or glue a piece of flannel or sandpaper to the back of the finished paper figure.

Goldilocks and the Three Bears

Literature References

Goldilocks: Classic Fairytales Pop-Ups Series, New York: Random House.

Goldilocks, adapted by Tom Roberts, illustrated by Laszlo Kubinyi. New York: Simon & Schuster, 1995. Cassette available. (Meg Ryan)

Goldilocks and the Three Bears, illustrated by Jan Brett. New York: Sandcastle Books (Putnam Publishing Group), 1990.

Goldilocks and the Three Bears, illustrated by Jonathan Langley. New York: HarperCollins, 1993.

Goldilocks and the Three Bears, illustrated by James Marshall. New York: Dial Books for Young Readers, 1988.

Goldilocks and the Three Bears, illustrated by David McPhail. New York: Scholastic, 1995.

Goldilocks and the Three Bears, illustrated by Laura Rader. New York: Tambourine Books (Morrow), 1995.

Goldilocks and the Three Bears: Lamb Chop's Play-Along Fairy Tales by Shari Lewis. New York: Bantam, 1994.

Materials: black, brown and tan paper; scissors; glue; black crayon or marker

Baby Bear

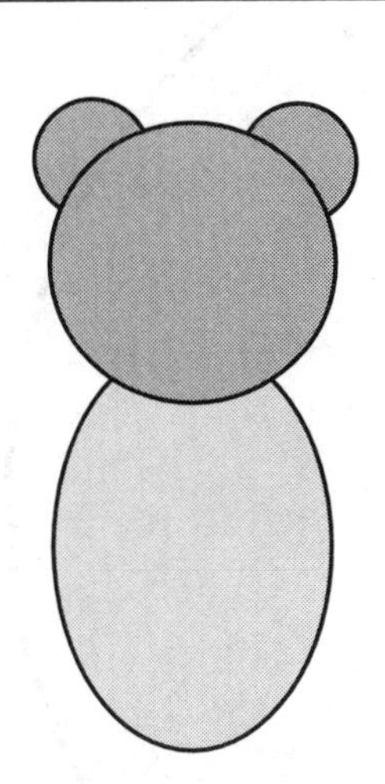

Cut one #1 head from brown paper. Cut two #2 ears from brown paper. Glue the ears to the back of the head as shown.

Cut one #3 body from tan paper. Glue the body to the back of the head as shown.

3 Cut four #4 arms/legs from brown paper. Glue them as shown to the back of the body.

4 Cut two #5 feet from brown paper. Glue the feet to the bottoms of the legs as shown.

5 Cut two #6 and six #7 paw prints from black paper. Glue on the feet as illustrated.

6 Cut two #8 eyes from black paper and glue on the head. Cut one #9 nose from black paper and glue in place as shown. With a black crayon or marker, draw the mouth and lines on the ears as shown.

BABY BEAR PATTERNS

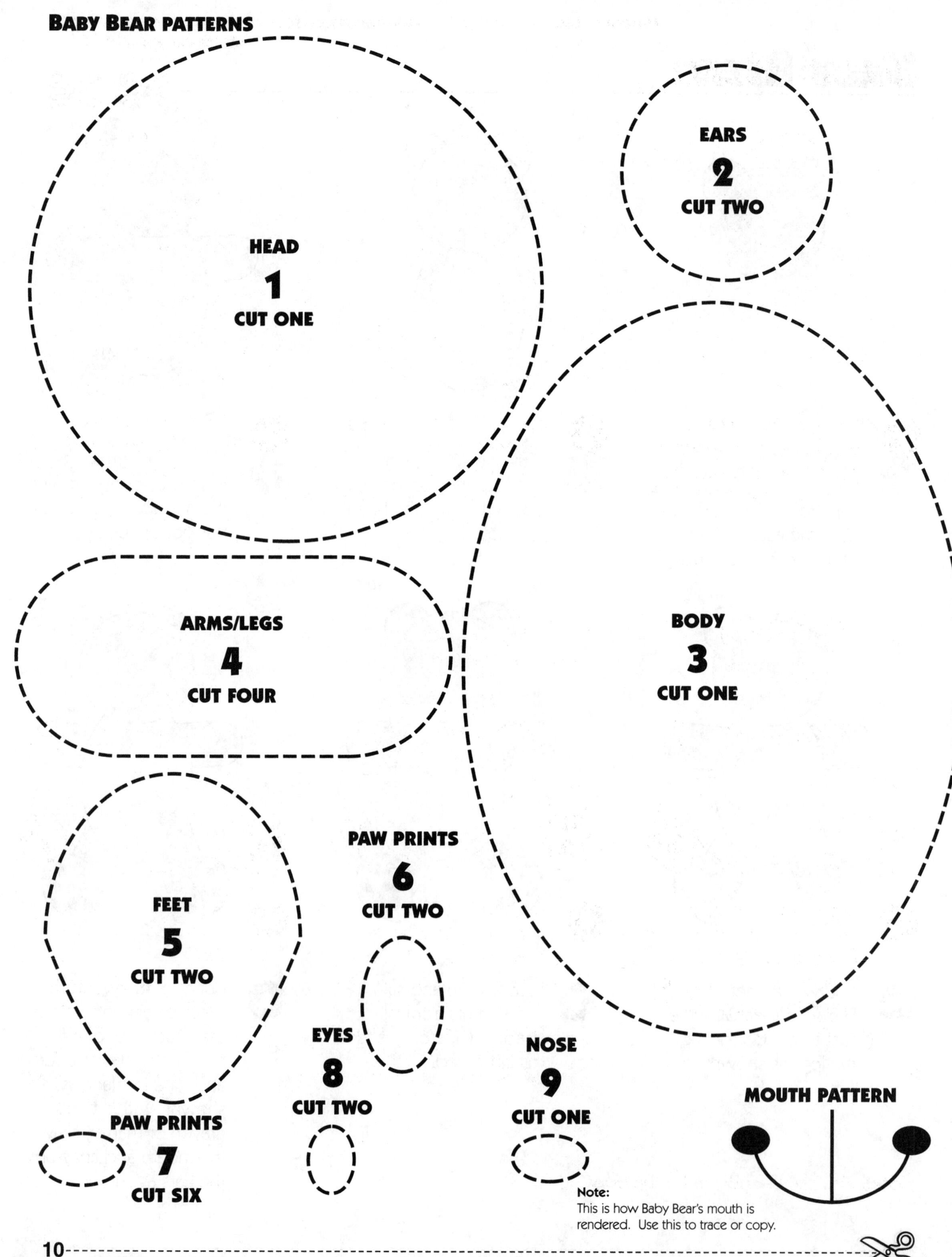

Note:
This is how Baby Bear's mouth is rendered. Use this to trace or copy.

Materials: *black, brown, red, tan and white paper; scissors; glue; black crayon or marker*
Optional Materials: *ribbon*

MAMA BEAR

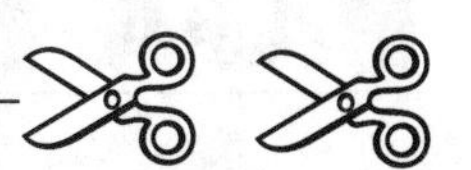

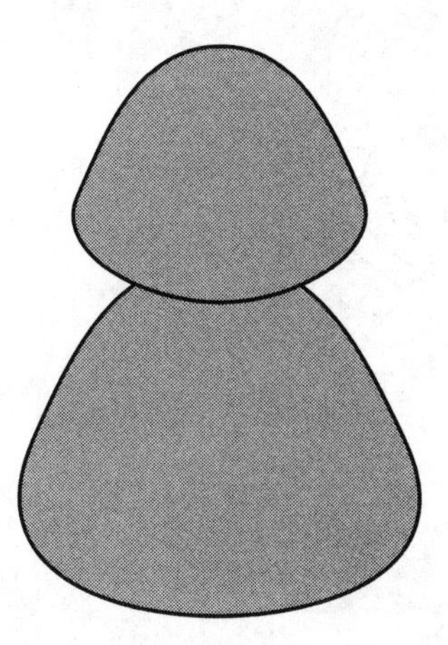

1 Cut one #1 body and one #2 head from brown paper. Glue the head to the top of the body.

2 Cut one #3 belly from tan paper and glue on the body. Cut two #4 ears from brown paper and glue to the back of the head as shown.

3 Cut two #5 arms from brown paper and glue in place as shown. Cut two #6 legs from brown paper and glue to the back of the body as illustrated.

 Cut two #7 feet from brown paper and glue on top of the legs. Cut two #8 and six #9 paw prints from black paper. Glue in place as shown.

5 Cut one #10 mouth from tan paper and glue on the head. Cut two #11 eyes from white paper. Cut two #12 pupils from black paper. Glue the pupils on the eyes; then glue the eyes on the head as illustrated.

6 Cut one #13 nose from black paper and glue as shown. With a black crayon or marker, draw the mouth and lines on the arms and ears as illustrated. Cut one #14 bow from red paper and glue to the top of the head as shown.

Note: You can use ribbon for the bow.

Materials: *black, brown, tan and white paper; scissors; glue; black crayon or marker*

PAPA BEAR

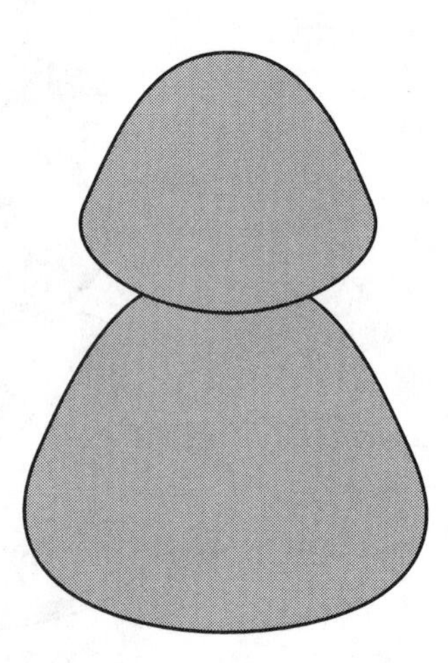

Cut one #1 body and one #2 head from brown paper. Glue the head to the top of the body.

Cut one #3 belly from tan paper and glue on the body. Cut two #4 ears from brown paper and glue to the back of the head as shown. Cut two #5 arms from brown paper and glue as shown. Cut two #6 legs from brown paper and glue to the back of the body as illustrated.

Cut two #7 feet from brown paper and glue on top of the legs. Cut one #10 mouth from tan paper and glue on the head. Cut two #15 eyes from white paper. Cut two #16 pupils from black paper. Glue the pupils on the eyes. Now glue the eyes on the head as illustrated.

4 Cut two #8 and six #9 paw prints from black paper. Glue in place as shown. Cut one #13 nose from black paper and glue on the mouth as illustrated.

With a black crayon or marker, draw the mouth and lines on the arms and ears as shown. Draw the bows of the glasses with black crayon or marker as shown.

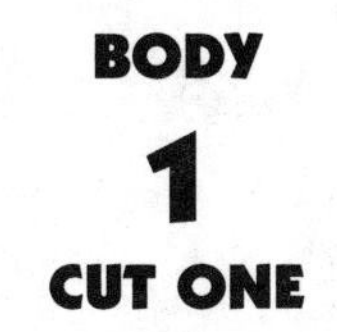
BODY
1
CUT ONE

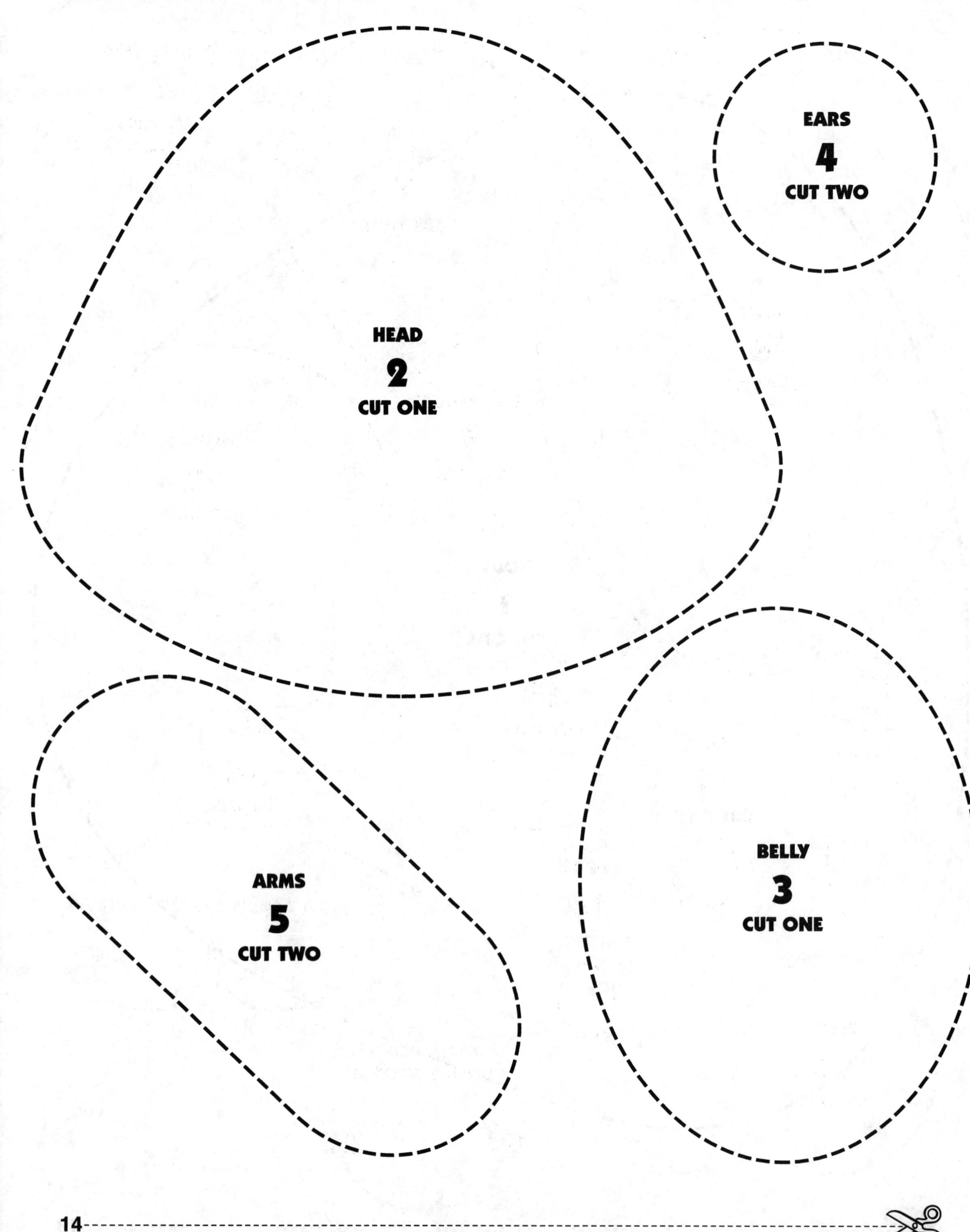
EARS
4
CUT TWO
HEAD
2
CUT ONE
ARMS
5
CUT TWO
BELLY
3
CUT ONE

Mama and Papa Bear patterns

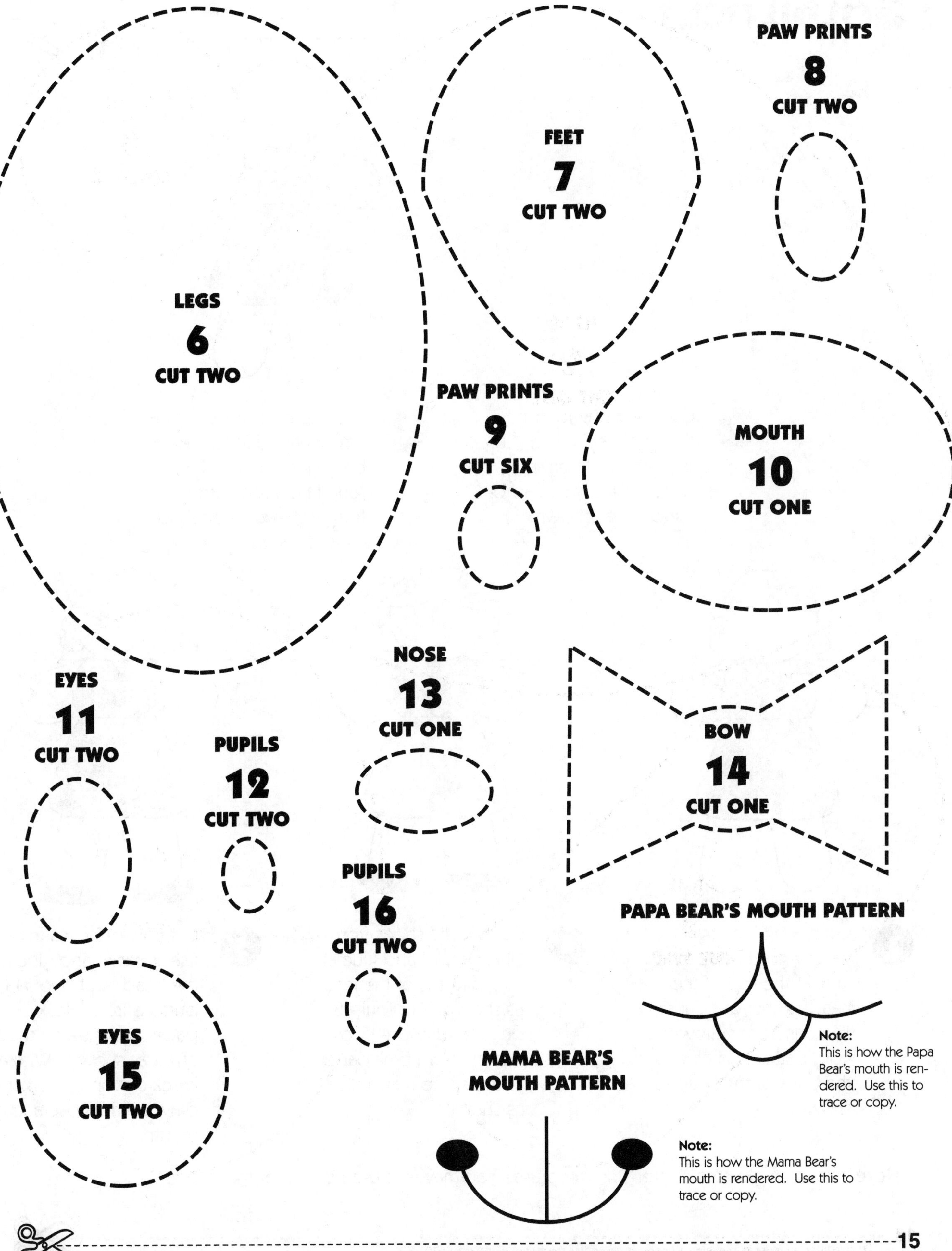

Materials: *black, flesh-colored, pink, white and yellow-gold paper; scissors; glue; black crayon or marker*
Optional Materials: *buttons, ribbon*

Goldilocks

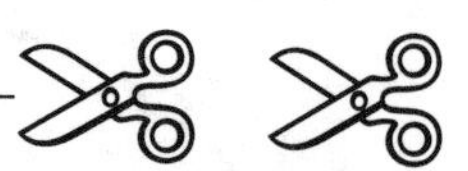

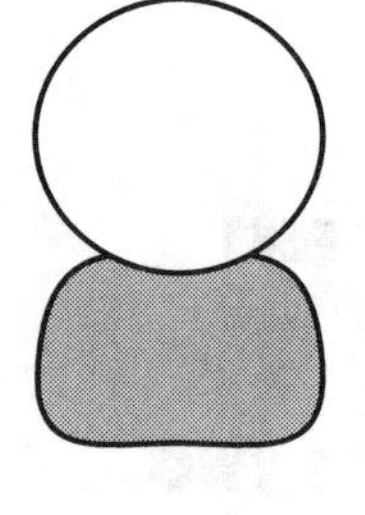

Cut one #1 head from flesh-colored paper. Cut one #2 chest from pink paper. Glue the head on the chest as shown.

Cut one #3 skirt from pink paper and glue to the back of the chest. Cut four #4 arms/legs from flesh-colored paper and glue as shown.

Cut two #5 hair from yellow-gold paper and glue at the top of the head as shown. Cut six #6 curls from yellow-gold paper and glue to the back of the head as shown.

4. Cut two #7 shoes from black paper and glue at the bottoms of the legs as shown. Cut four #8 bows and two #9 bow centers from pink paper and assemble and glue as shown.

5. Cut two #10 eyes from black paper and glue on the head. Cut two #11 buttons from black paper and glue on the chest as shown. With a black crayon or marker, draw on the nose and mouth.

Note: You can glue real buttons on the dress. You may also use ribbon for the bows.

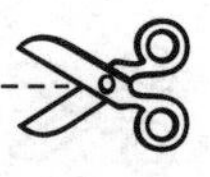

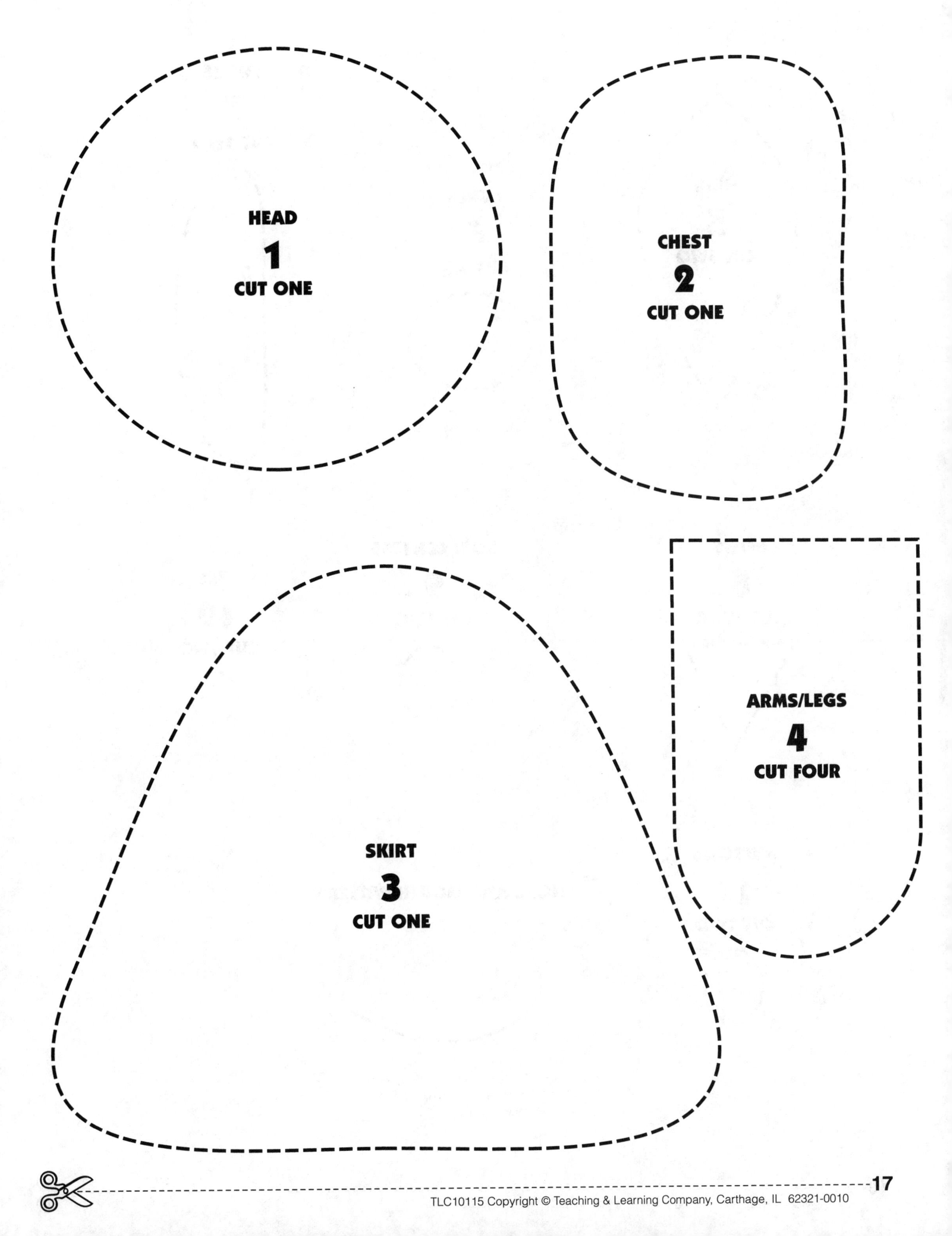
HEAD
1
CUT ONE
CHEST
2
CUT ONE
SKIRT
3
CUT ONE
ARMS/LEGS
4
CUT FOUR

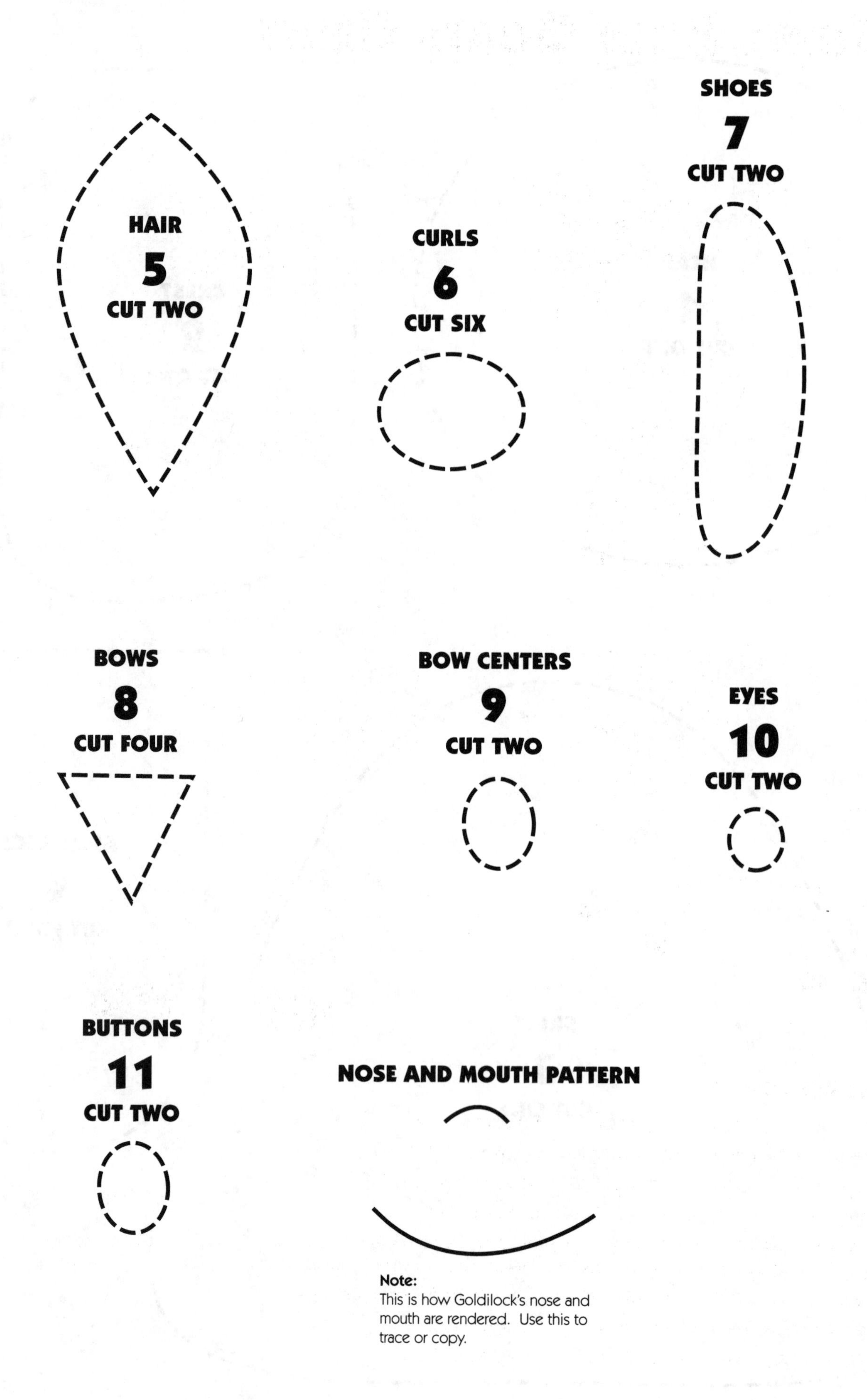

Note:
This is how Goldilock's nose and mouth are rendered. Use this to trace or copy.

The Three Billy Goats Gruff

Literature References

Three Billy Goats Gruff, by Ellen Appleby, New York: Scholastic, 1985.

Three Billy Goats Gruff, by Tom Arnold, New York: Simon & Schuster Childrens, 1993.

Three Billy Goats Gruff, by Robert Bender, New York: Henry Holt & Co., 1993.

Three Billy Goats Gruff, by Paul Galdone, New York: Scholastic, 1989.

Three Billy Goats Gruff, adapted by Tom Roberts, illustrated by David Jorgensen, Racine, WI: Golden Press (Western Publishing), 1993. Read by Holly Hunter (audio). Rabbit Ears Storybook Classic Series.

Three Billy Goats Gruff, by Sue Kassirer, New York: Random Books for Young Readers.

Three Billy Goats Gruff, by Glenn Rounds, New York: Holiday, 1993.

Three Billy Goats Gruff, by Janet Stevens, Orlando, FL: HarBrace, 1987.

Materials: *black, blue, brown, light green and white paper; scissors; glue; black crayon or marker*

TROLL

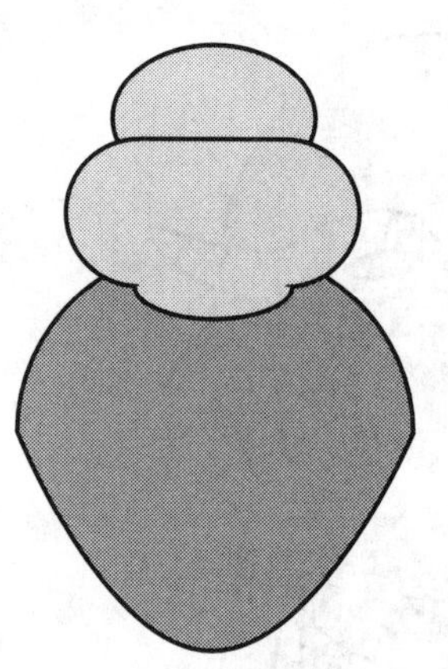

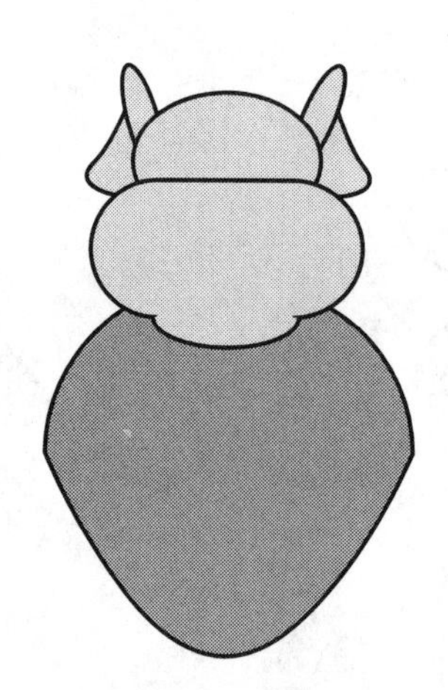

1. Cut one #1 body from blue paper. Cut one #2 head and one #3 face from light green paper and glue as shown.

2. Cut two #4 outer ears and two #5 ears from light green paper. Glue the ears on the head as shown.

3. Cut one #6 snout and two #7 nosepieces from light green paper and glue on the face as shown. Cut four #8 arms from light green paper and glue as illustrated.

4. Cut two #9 hands from light green paper and glue at the ends of the arms as illustrated. Cut one #10 club from brown paper and glue on one hand.

5. Cut two #11 thighs and two #12 legs from brown paper and glue as shown. Cut two #13 feet from black paper and glue at the bottoms of the legs. Cut four #14 fingers from light green paper and glue on top of the club as shown.

6. Cut two #15 eyes from white paper. Cut two #16 pupils from black paper. Glue the pupils on the eyes. Cut two #17 eyelids from light green paper and glue on the eyes as shown. Now glue the assembled eyes on the head. Use a black crayon or marker to draw the mouth, teeth, ear lines, hair and fingers of the other hand.

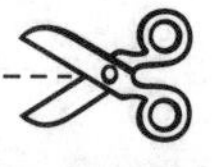

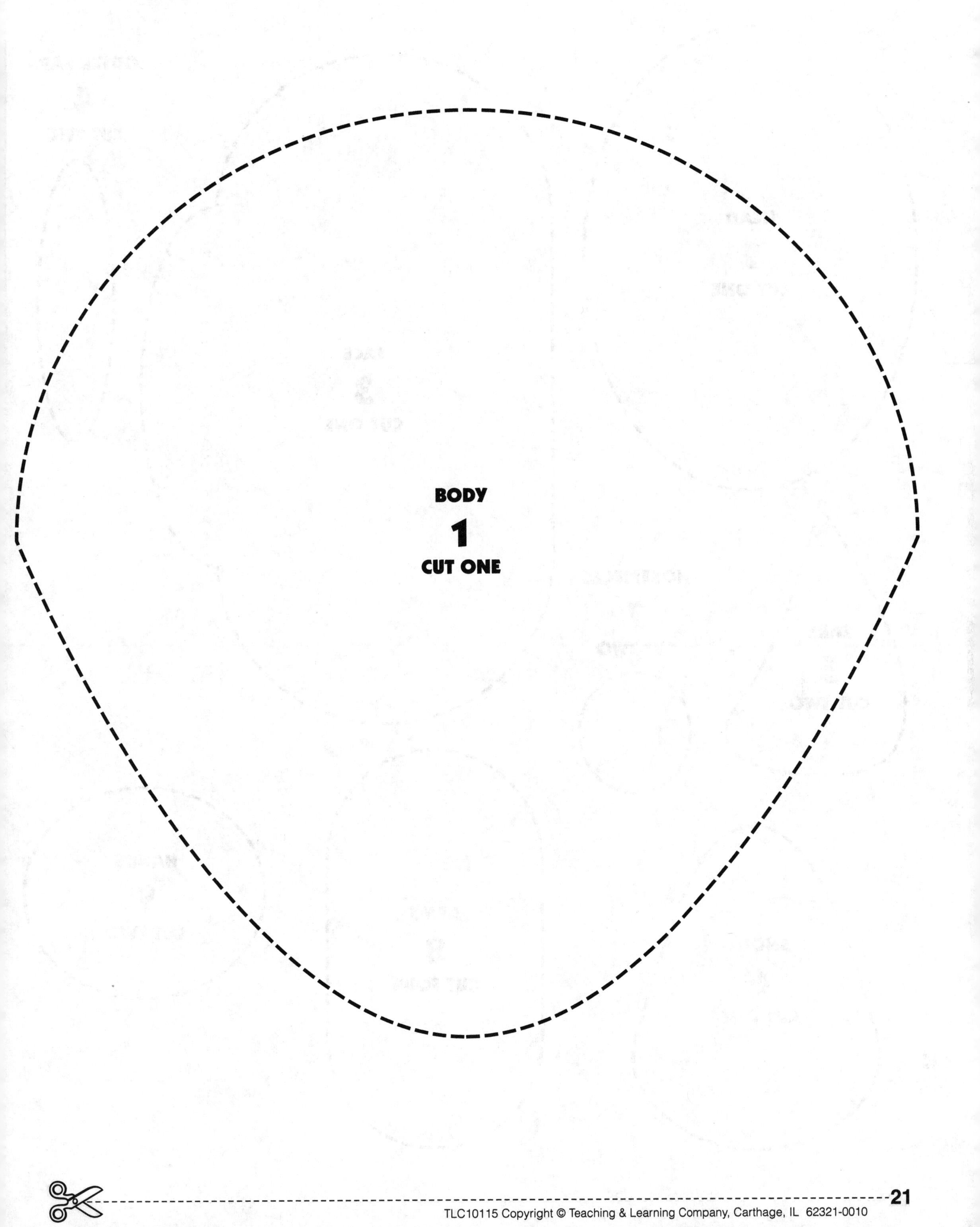
BODY
1
CUT ONE

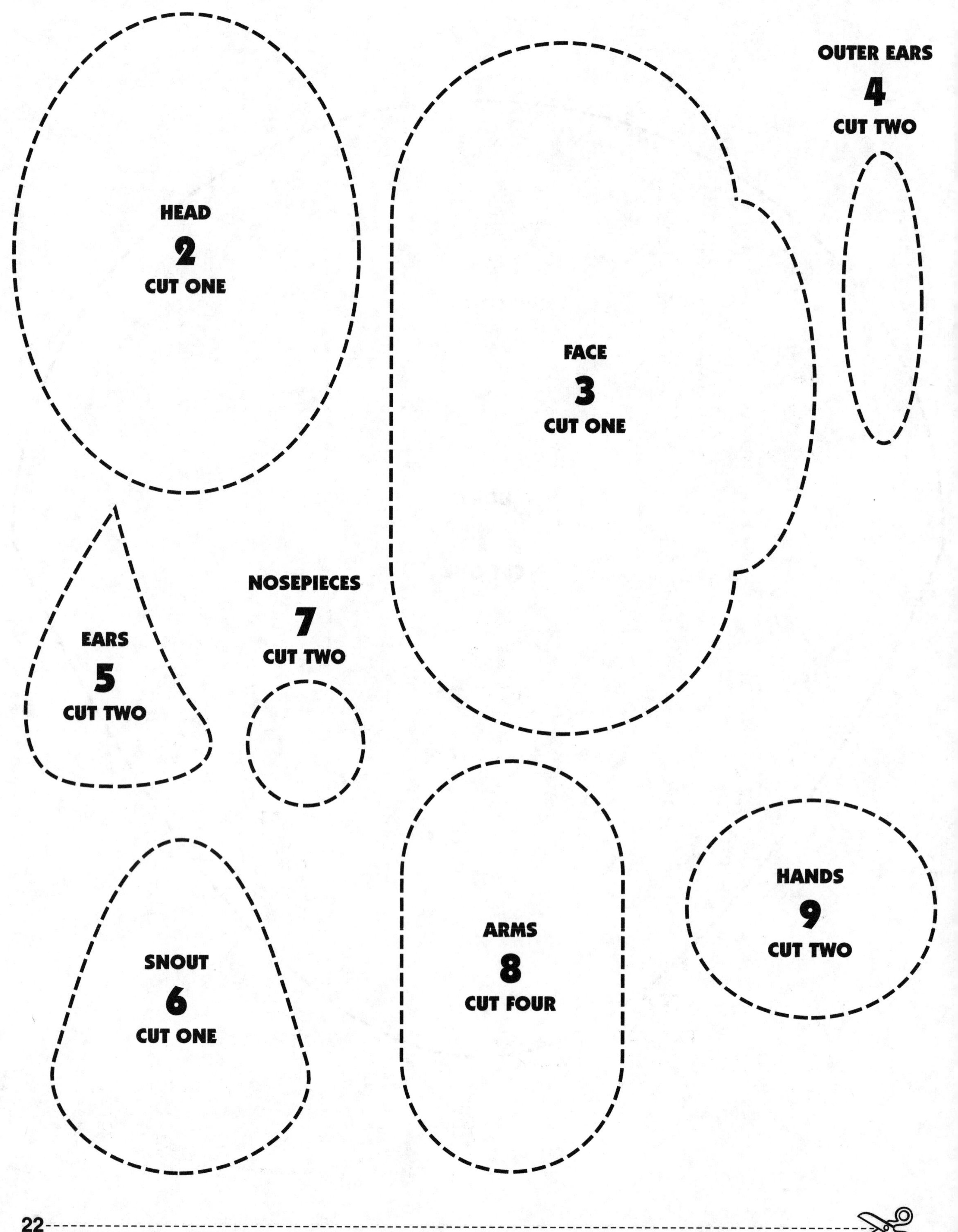
HEAD
2
CUT ONE
FACE
3
CUT ONE
OUTER EARS
4
CUT TWO
EARS
5
CUT TWO
NOSEPIECES
7
CUT TWO
SNOUT
6
CUT ONE
ARMS
8
CUT FOUR
HANDS
9
CUT TWO

TROLL PATTERNS

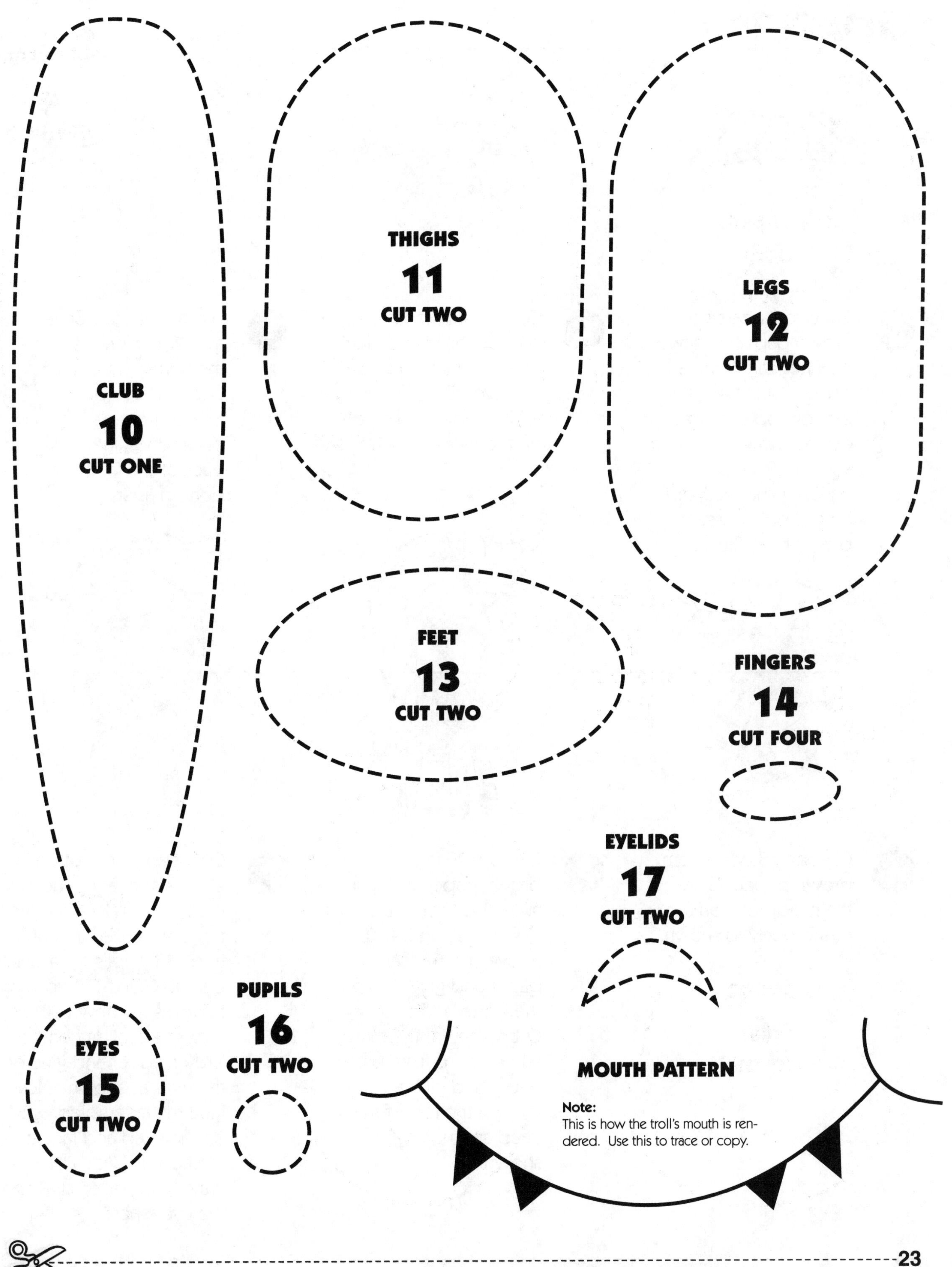

Materials: *black, brown, dark brown, tan and white paper; scissors; glue; black crayon or marker*

Goat 1

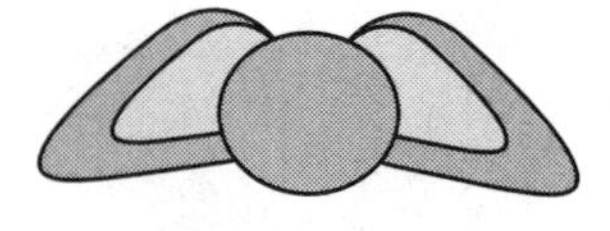

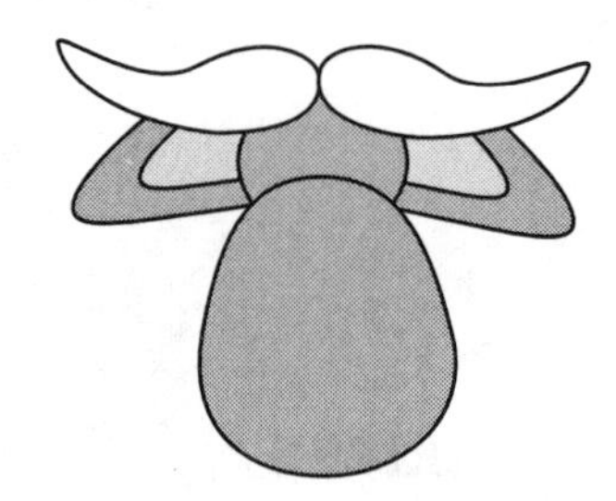

1 Cut two #1 ears from brown paper. Cut two #2 inner ears from tan paper. Glue the inner ears on top of the #1 ears as shown. Cut one #3 head from brown paper. Glue the head on top of the assembled ears as illustrated.

2 Cut one #4 face from brown paper and glue to the front of the head. Cut two #5 horns from white paper and glue on the ears and head as shown.

3 Use a black crayon or marker to draw lines on the horns. Cut one #6 beard and two #7 beards from dark brown paper and glue to the back of the face at the bottom as shown.

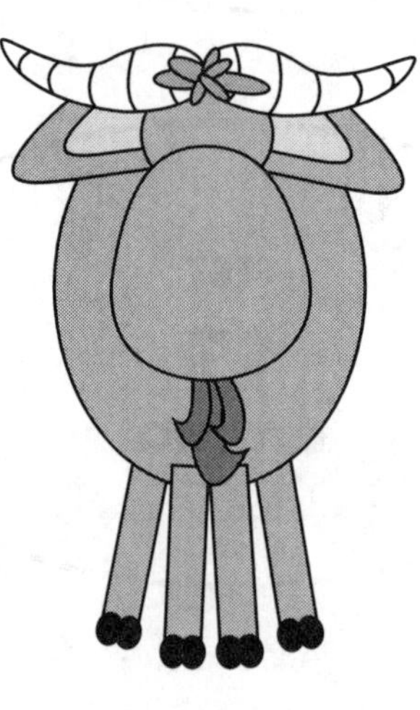

4 Cut one #8 body from brown paper. Glue the headpiece on top of the body as shown.

5 Cut four #9 legs from brown paper and glue at the bottom of the body. Cut eight #10 hooves from black paper and glue two on the bottom of each leg. Cut several of the three hair patterns from brown paper and glue a fore-lock on the top of the head and horns as shown.

6 Cut one #11 nose from black paper and glue in place. Cut two #12 eyes from white paper. Cut two #13 pupils from black paper. Glue the pupils on the eyes as shown. Cut two #14 eyelids from brown paper and glue on the eyes as shown. Now glue the assembled eyes on the head and face as illustrated. With a black crayon or marker, draw on the eyelashes.

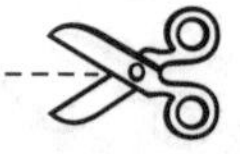

Materials: *black, dark brown, gray, tan and white paper; scissors; glue; black crayon or marker*

GOAT 2

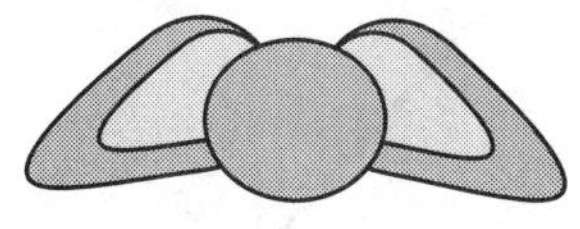

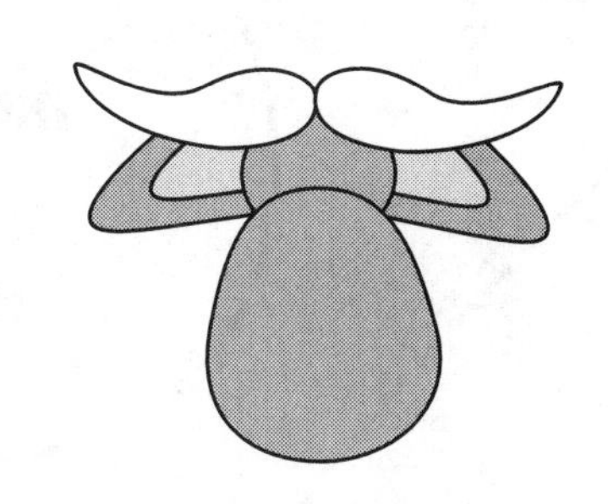

1 Cut two #1 ears from brown paper. Cut two #2 inner ears from tan paper. Glue the inner ears on top of the #1 ears as shown. Cut one #3 head from brown paper. Glue the head on top of the assembled ears as illustrated.

2 Cut one #4 face from brown paper and glue to the front of the head. Cut two #5 horns from white paper and glue on the ears and head as shown.

3 Use a black crayon or marker to draw lines on the horns. Cut one #6 beard and two #7 beards from dark brown paper and glue to the back of the face at the bottom as shown.

4 Cut one #8 body from gray paper. Glue the headpiece on top of the body as shown.

5 Cut four #9 legs from gray paper and glue at the bottom of the body as shown. Cut eight #10 hooves from black paper and glue two on the bottom of each leg. Cut several of the three hair patterns from gray paper and glue a forelock on the top of the head and horns as shown.

6 Cut one #11 nose from black paper and glue in place. Cut two #12 eyes from white paper. Cut two #13 pupils from black paper. Glue the pupils on the eyes as shown. Cut two #14 eyelids from brown paper and glue on the eyes as shown. Now glue the assembled eyes on the head and face as illustrated. With a black crayon or marker, draw on the eyelashes.

GOATS 1 AND 2 PATTERNS

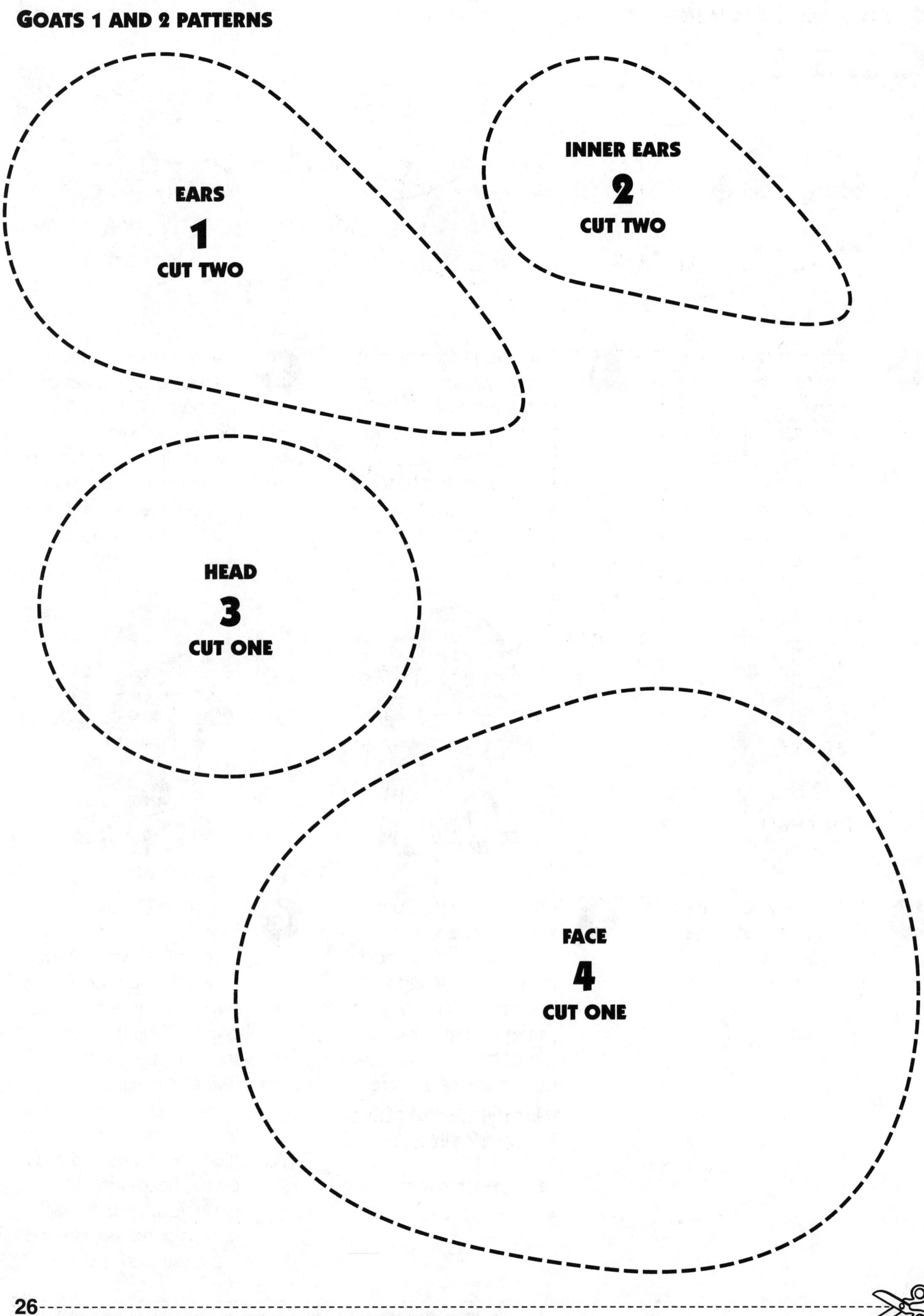

Goats 1 and 2 Patterns

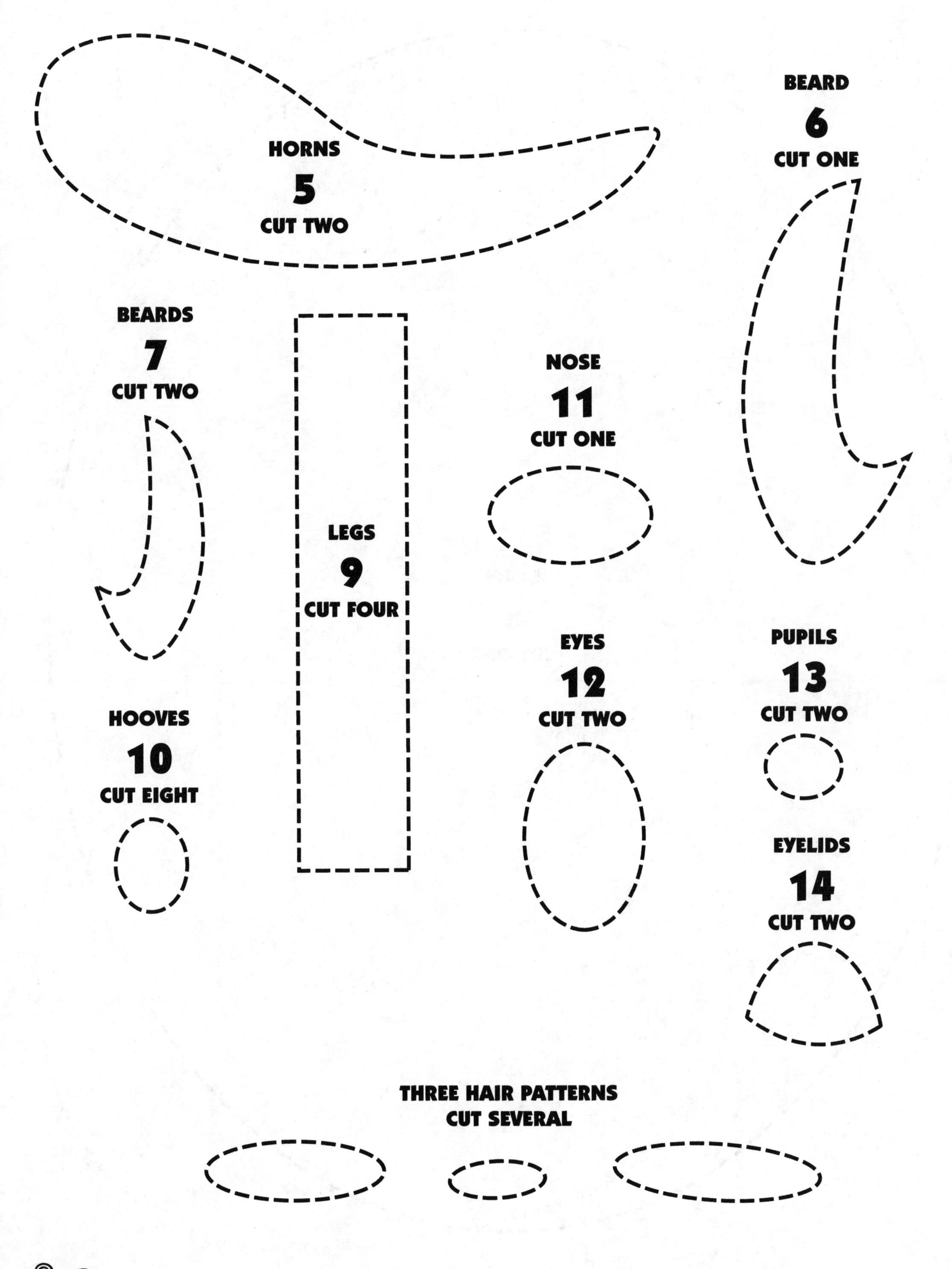

BODY

8

CUT ONE

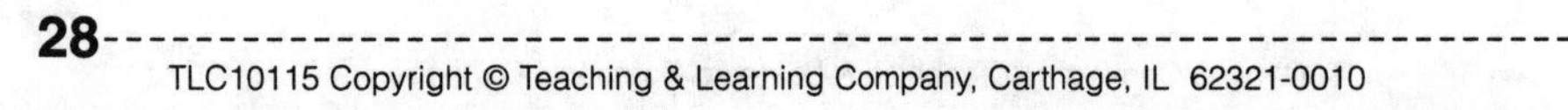

Materials: *black, off-white, pink, tan and white paper; scissors; glue; black crayon or marker*

GOAT 3

1 Cut one #1 body and one #2 neck from off-white paper. Glue the body to the neck as shown.

2 Cut one #3 head from off-white paper and glue at the top of the neck. Cut two #4 horns from white paper and glue to the back of the head as shown.

3 Cut one #5 face from off-white paper. Cut one #6 ear from off-white paper and glue on the head as shown. Use a black crayon or marker to draw lines on the horns.

4 Cut one #7 inner ear from pink paper and glue on top of the #6 ear. Cut one #8 hip from off-white paper and glue at the back of the body as illustrated. Cut one #9 beard and two #10 beards from tan paper and glue to the bottom of the face as shown.

5 Cut three #11 legs and two #12 legs from off-white paper and glue on the legs as shown. Cut eight #13 hooves from black paper and glue two on the bottom of each leg. Cut one #14 tail from off-white paper and glue to the back of the body. Cut several of the three hair patterns from off-white paper and glue a forelock on top of the head and horns as shown.

6 Cut one #15 nose from black paper and glue on the face as illustrated. Cut one #16 eye from white paper. Cut one #17 pupil from black paper. Glue the pupil on the eye. Cut one #18 eyelid from off-white paper and glue on the eye as shown. Now glue the assembled eye on the head and face as shown. With a black crayon or marker, draw on eyelashes and the lines on the tail.

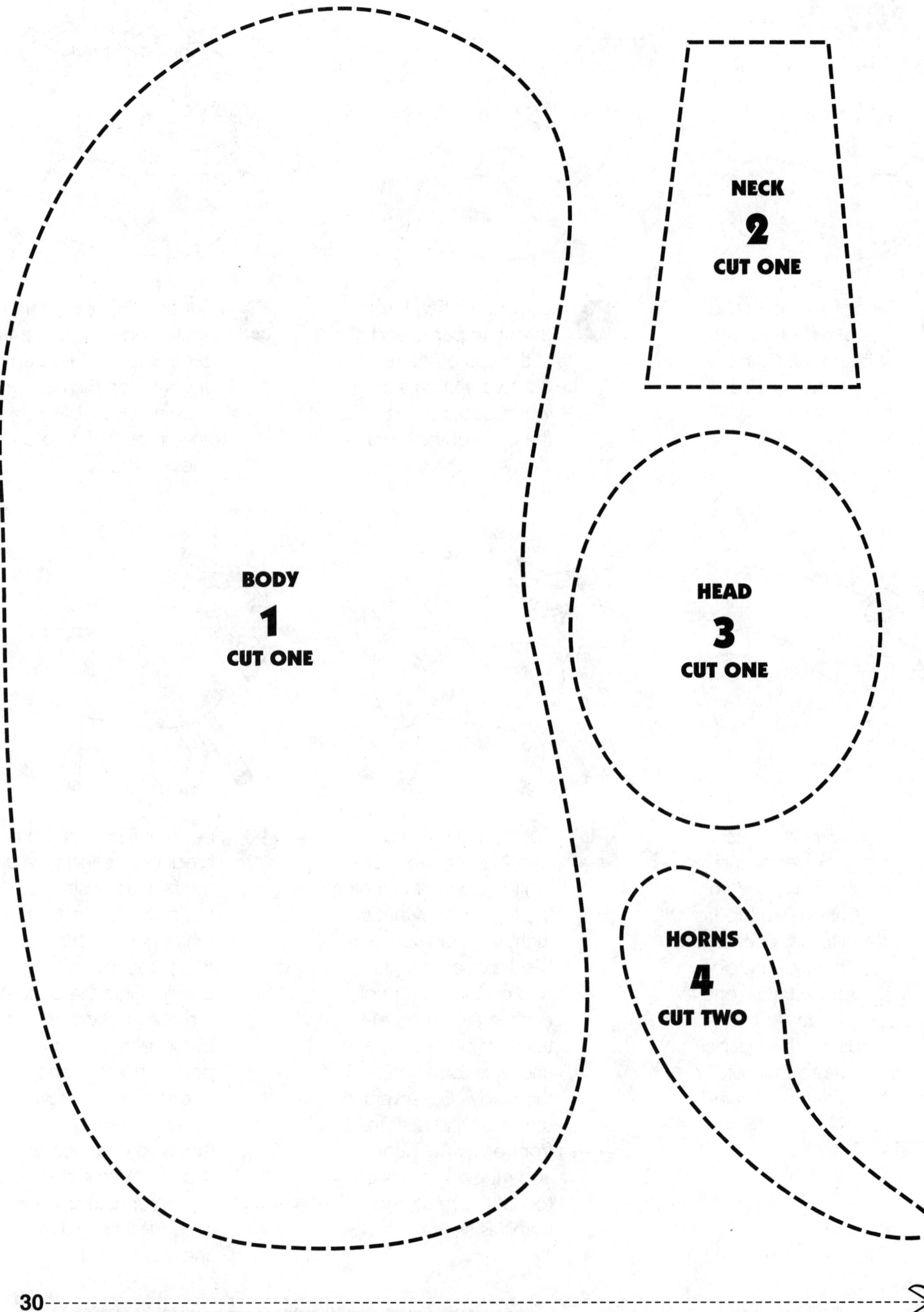
NECK
2
CUT ONE
BODY
1
CUT ONE
HEAD
3
CUT ONE
HORNS
4
CUT TWO

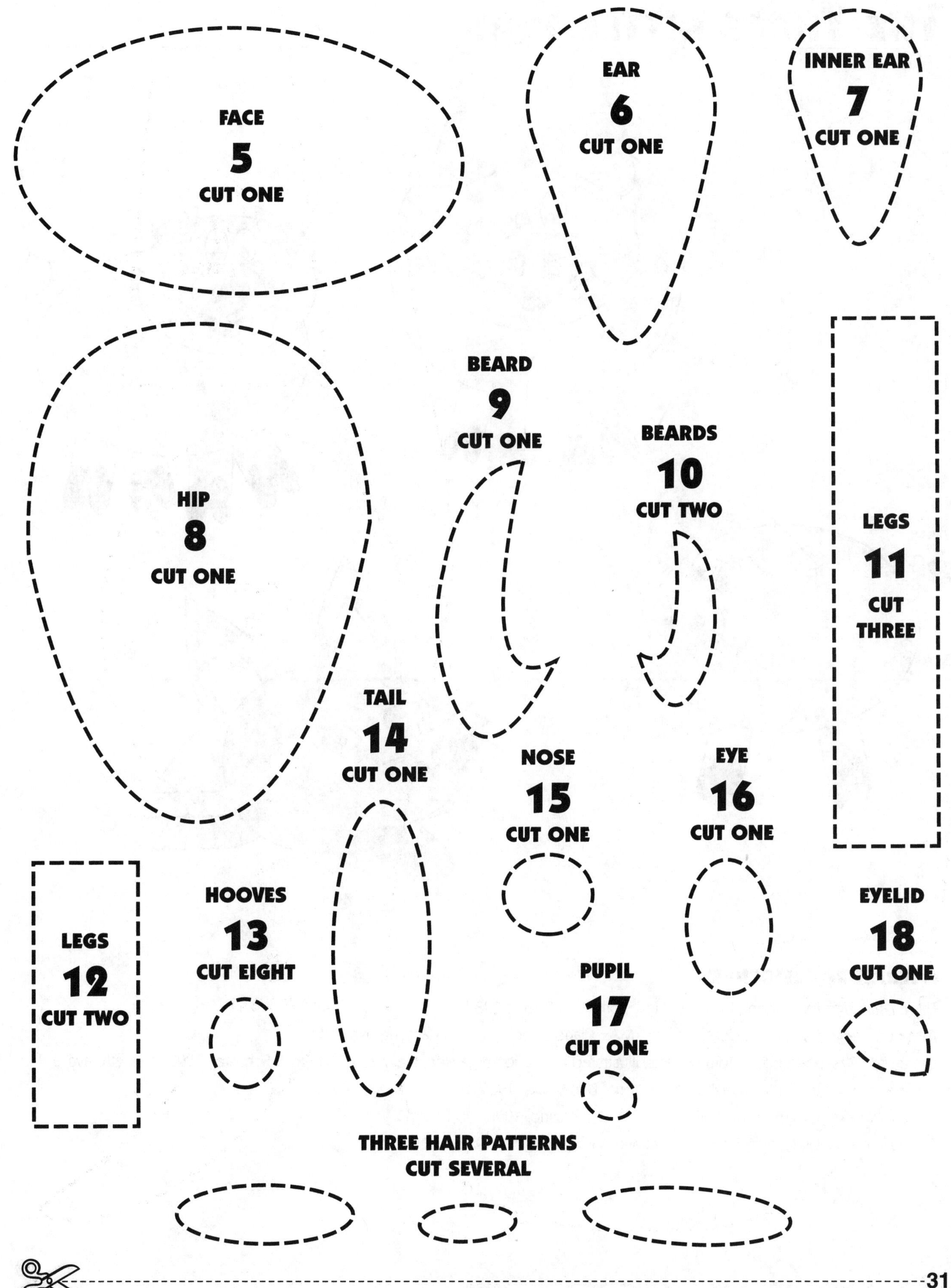
FACE
5
CUT ONE
EAR
6
CUT ONE
INNER EAR
7
CUT ONE
HIP
8
CUT ONE
BEARD
9
CUT ONE
BEARDS
10
CUT TWO
LEGS
11
CUT THREE
TAIL
14
CUT ONE
NOSE
15
CUT ONE
EYE
16
CUT ONE
LEGS
12
CUT TWO
HOOVES
13
CUT EIGHT
PUPIL
17
CUT ONE
EYELID
18
CUT ONE
THREE HAIR PATTERNS
CUT SEVERAL

The Three Little Pigs

Literature References

Three Little Pigs, by Caroline Bucknall, New York: Dial Books, 1987.

Three Little Pigs, by Paul Galdone, Boston, MA: Clarion Books, 1979. Cassette available.

Three Little Pigs, adapted by Tom Roberts, illustrated by David Jorgensen, New York: Simon & Schuster, 1993. Cassette available.

Three Little Pigs, by James Marshall, New York: Dial Books, 1989.

Three Little Pigs, by David McPhail, New York: Scholastic, 1995.

Three Little Pigs, by Harriet Ziefert, New York: Viking Penguin, 1995.

Materials: *black, dark pink, light pink and white paper; scissors; glue; black crayon or marker*
Optional Materials: *wiggly eyes*

PIG 1

1. Cut one #1 body from light pink paper.
2. Cut two #2 ears from dark pink paper and glue to the body as shown.
3. Cut two #3 ears from dark pink paper and glue on the tops of the #2 ears as illustrated.
4. Cut one #4 nose from dark pink paper and glue in place. Cut one each of #5, #6 and #7 tail pieces from dark pink paper and assemble and glue as shown.
5. Cut two #8 legs from light pink paper and glue to the back of the body. Cut four #9 hooves from black paper and glue two at the bottom of each leg as shown.
6. Cut two #10 eyes from white paper. Cut two #11 pupils from black paper. Glue the pupils on the eyes. Now glue on the assembled eyes as shown. Cut two #12 nostrils from black paper and glue to the nose.

Note: You may use wiggly eyes.

PIG 1 PATTERNS

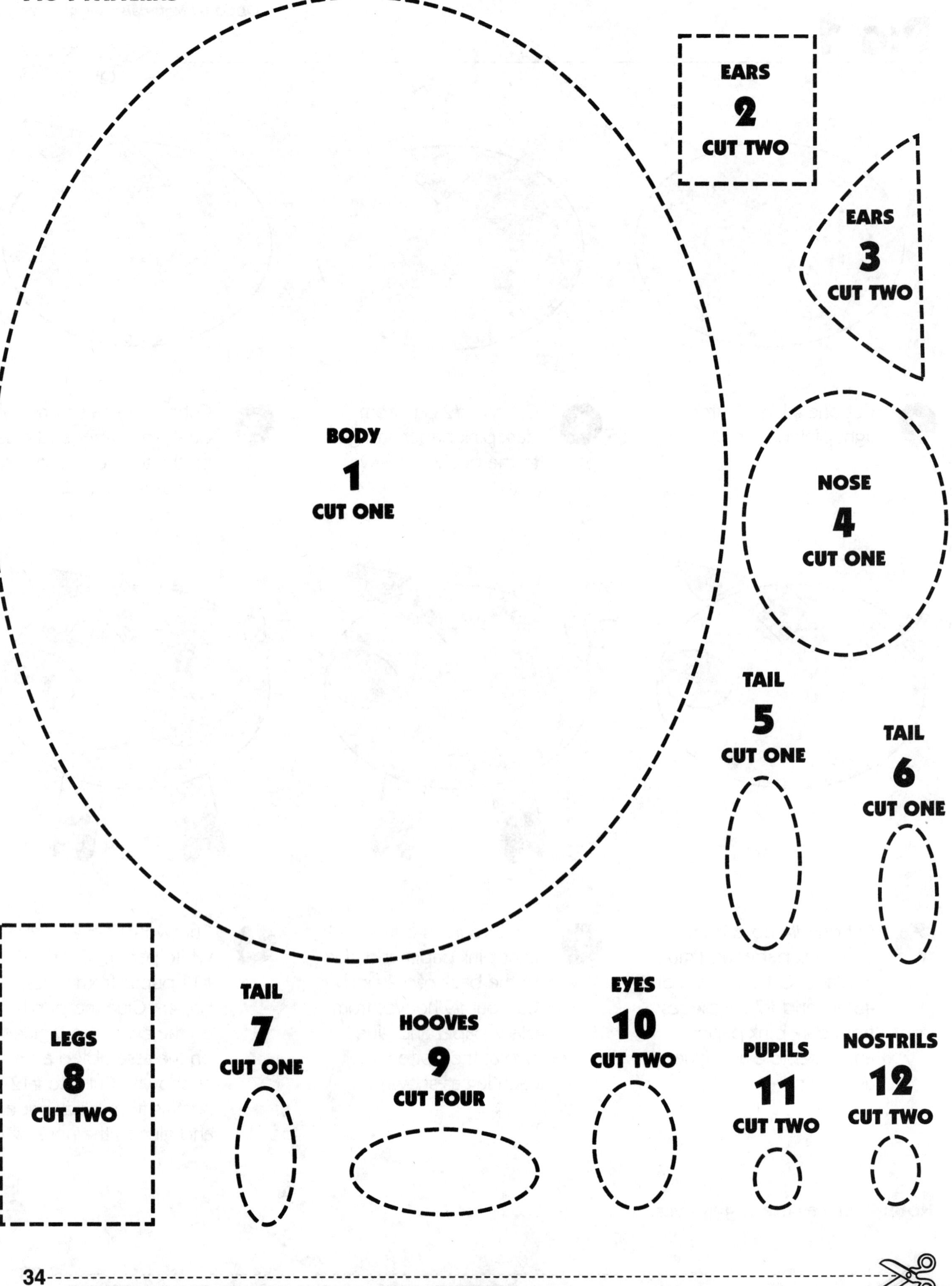
BODY
1
CUT ONE
EARS
2
CUT TWO
EARS
3
CUT TWO
NOSE
4
CUT ONE
TAIL
5
CUT ONE
TAIL
6
CUT ONE
LEGS
8
CUT TWO
TAIL
7
CUT ONE
HOOVES
9
CUT FOUR
EYES
10
CUT TWO
PUPILS
11
CUT TWO
NOSTRILS
12
CUT TWO

Materials: *black, dark pink, light pink, red and white paper; scissors; glue; black crayon or marker*
Optional Materials: *pipe cleaner or yarn, wiggly eyes*

PIG 2

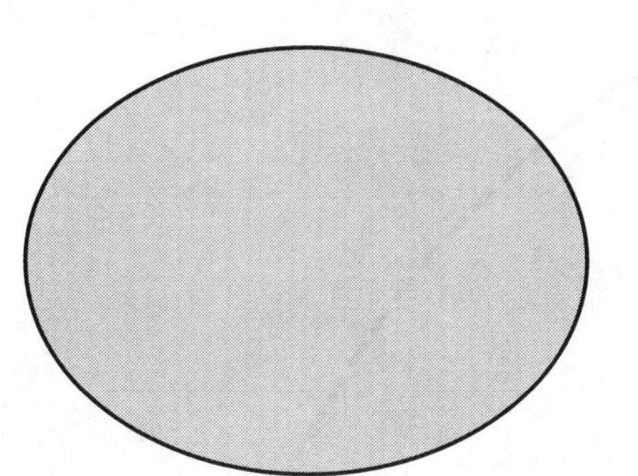

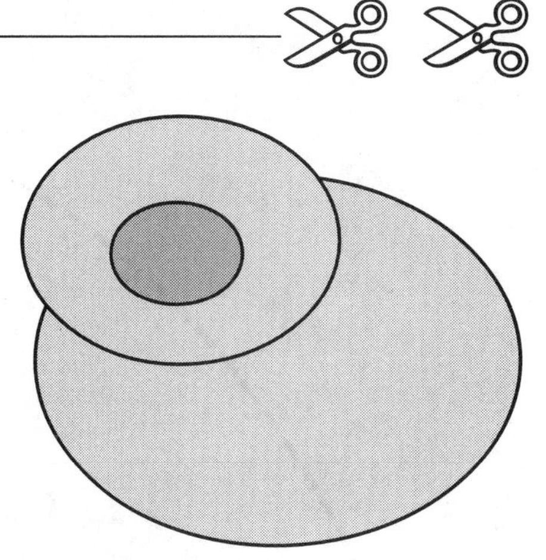

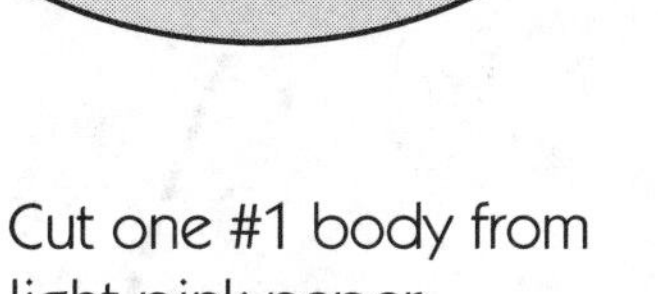

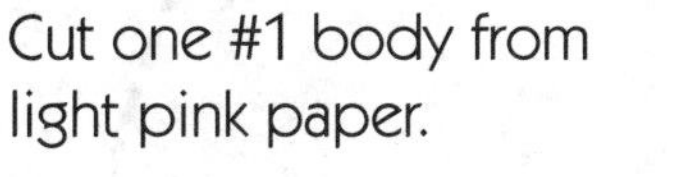

1. Cut one #1 body from light pink paper.

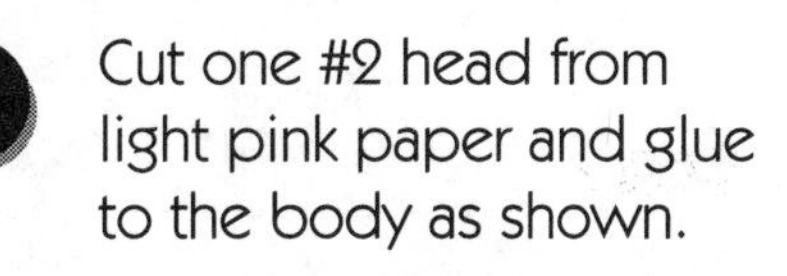

2. Cut one #2 head from light pink paper and glue to the body as shown.

3. Cut one #3 nose from dark pink paper and glue in place.

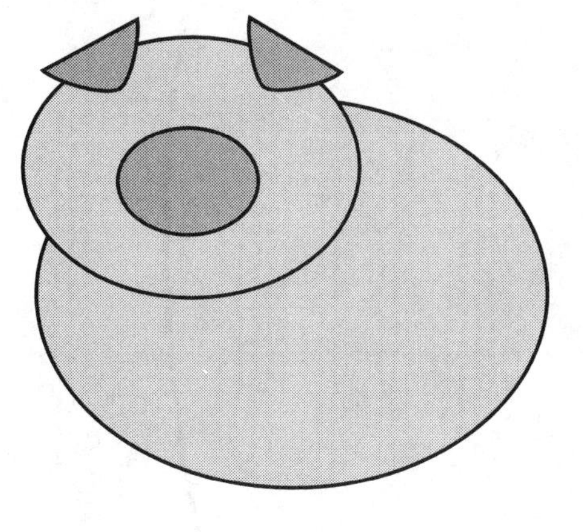

4. Cut two #4 ears from dark pink paper and glue at the top of the head as illustrated.

5. Cut four #5 legs from light pink paper and glue to the back of the body. Cut eight #6 hooves from black paper and glue two at the bottom of each leg. Cut two #7 nostrils from black paper and glue on the nose.

6. Cut two #8 eyes from white paper. Cut two #9 pupils from black paper. Glue the pupils on the eyes. Now glue the assembled eyes on the head as shown. Cut one #10 tongue from red paper and glue to the bottom of the nose. With a black crayon or marker, draw on the mouth. Add a tail by gluing on a twisted pipe cleaner or a length of yarn.

Note: You may use wiggly eyes.

BODY

1

CUT ONE

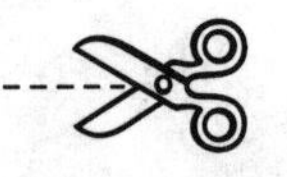

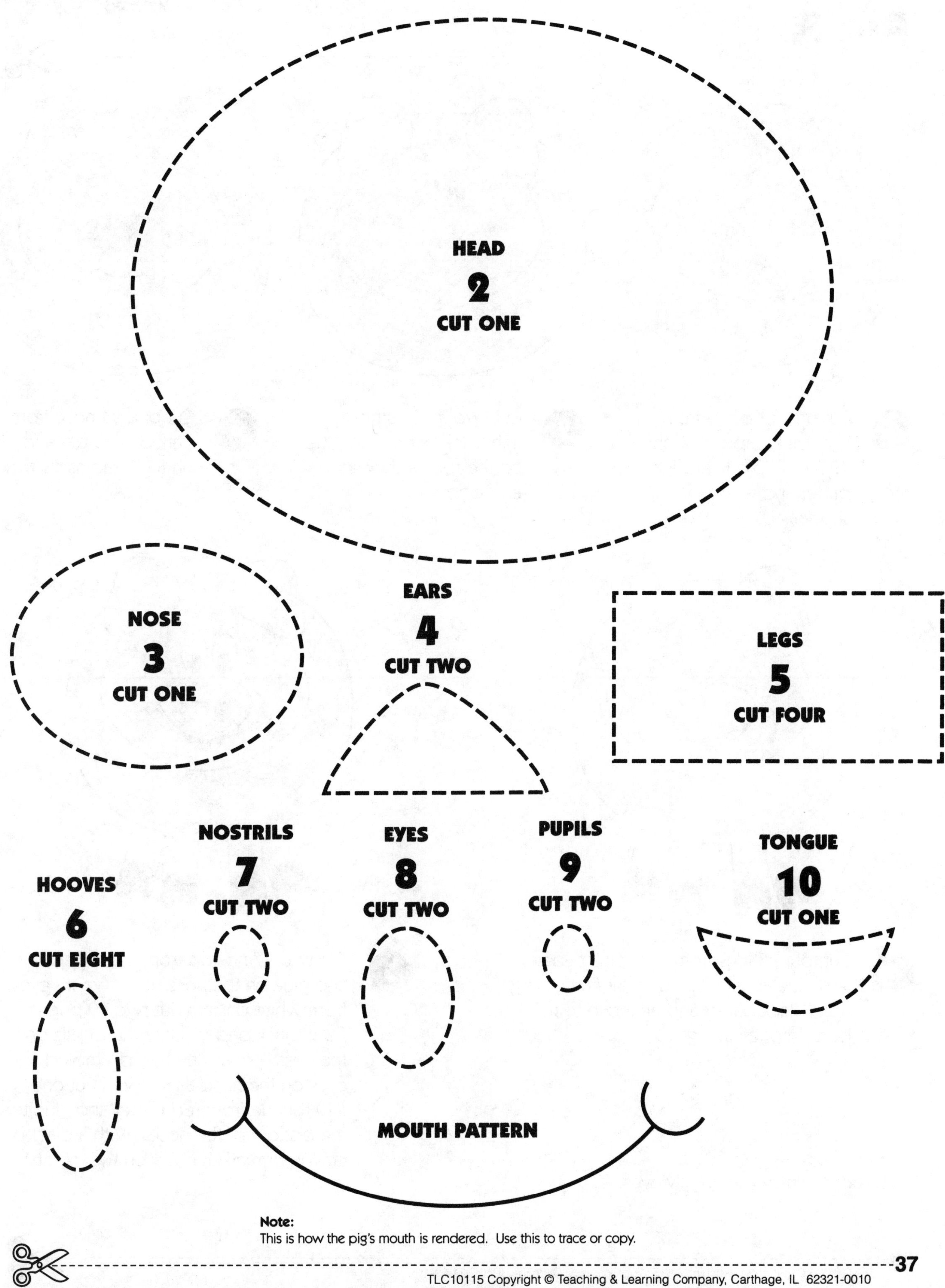

Note:
This is how the pig's mouth is rendered. Use this to trace or copy.

Materials: *black, dark pink, light pink, pink, red and white paper; scissors; glue; black crayon or marker*
Optional Materials: *wiggly eyes*

Pig 3

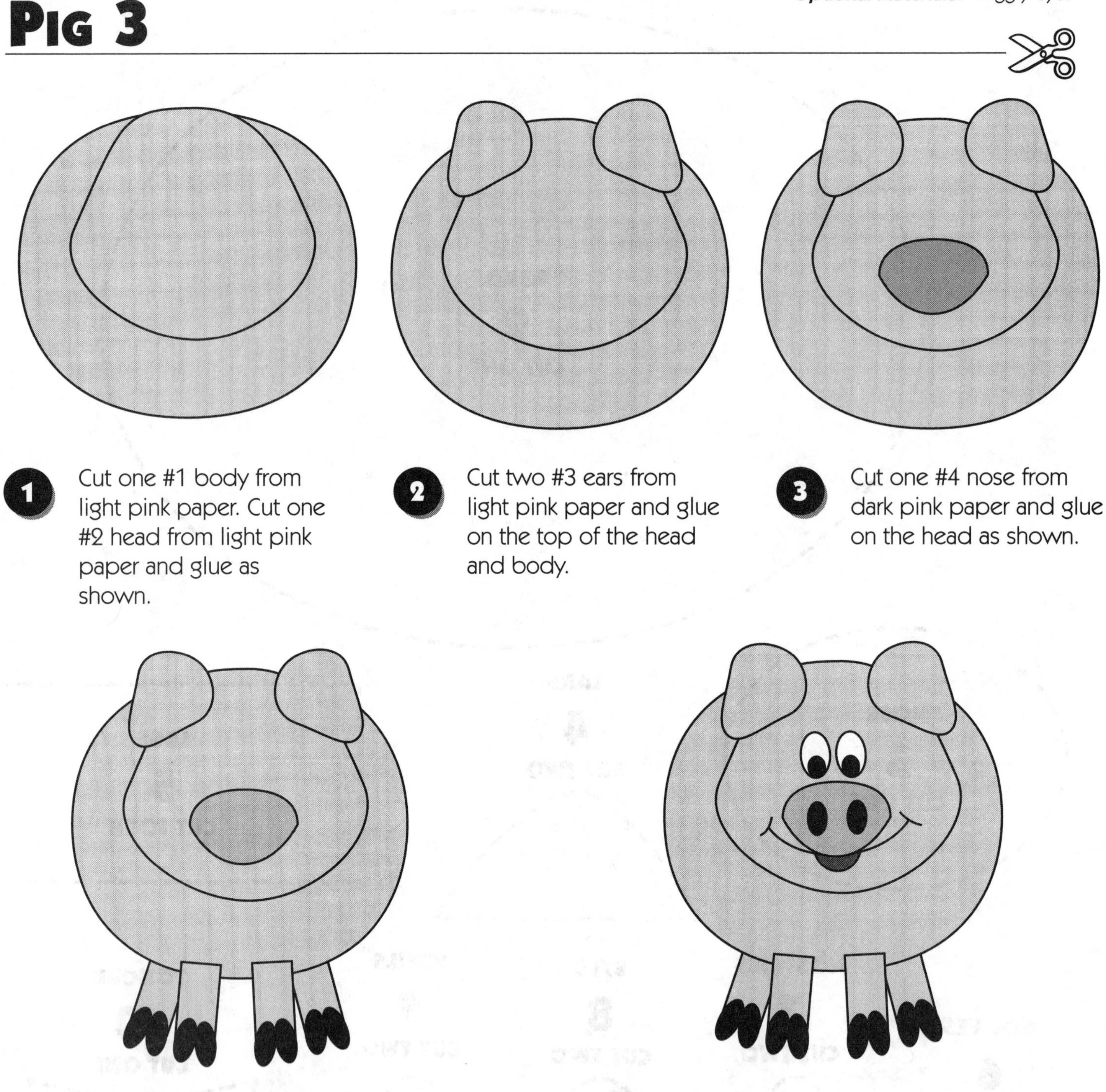

1. Cut one #1 body from light pink paper. Cut one #2 head from light pink paper and glue as shown.

2. Cut two #3 ears from light pink paper and glue on the top of the head and body.

3. Cut one #4 nose from dark pink paper and glue on the head as shown.

4. Cut four #5 legs from light pink paper and glue as shown. Cut eight #6 hooves from black paper and glue two to the bottom of each leg.

5. Cut two #7 nostrils from black paper and glue on the nose. Cut two #8 eyes from white paper. Cut two #9 pupils from black paper. Glue the pupils on the eyes. Now glue the assembled eyes on the head as shown. Cut one #10 tongue from red paper and glue to the bottom of the nose. With a black crayon or marker, draw on the mouth.

Note: You may use wiggly eyes.

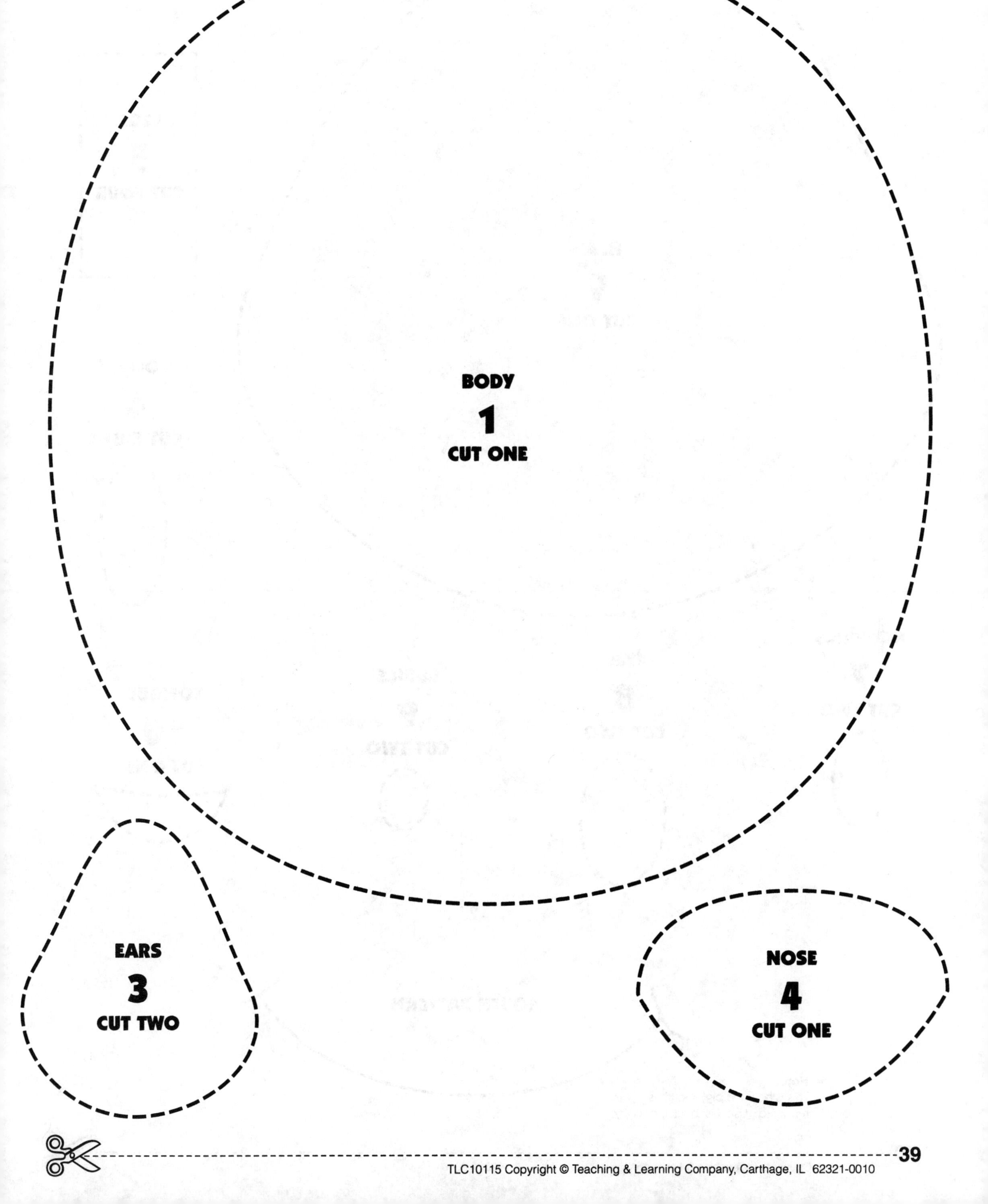
BODY
1
CUT ONE
EARS
3
CUT TWO
NOSE
4
CUT ONE

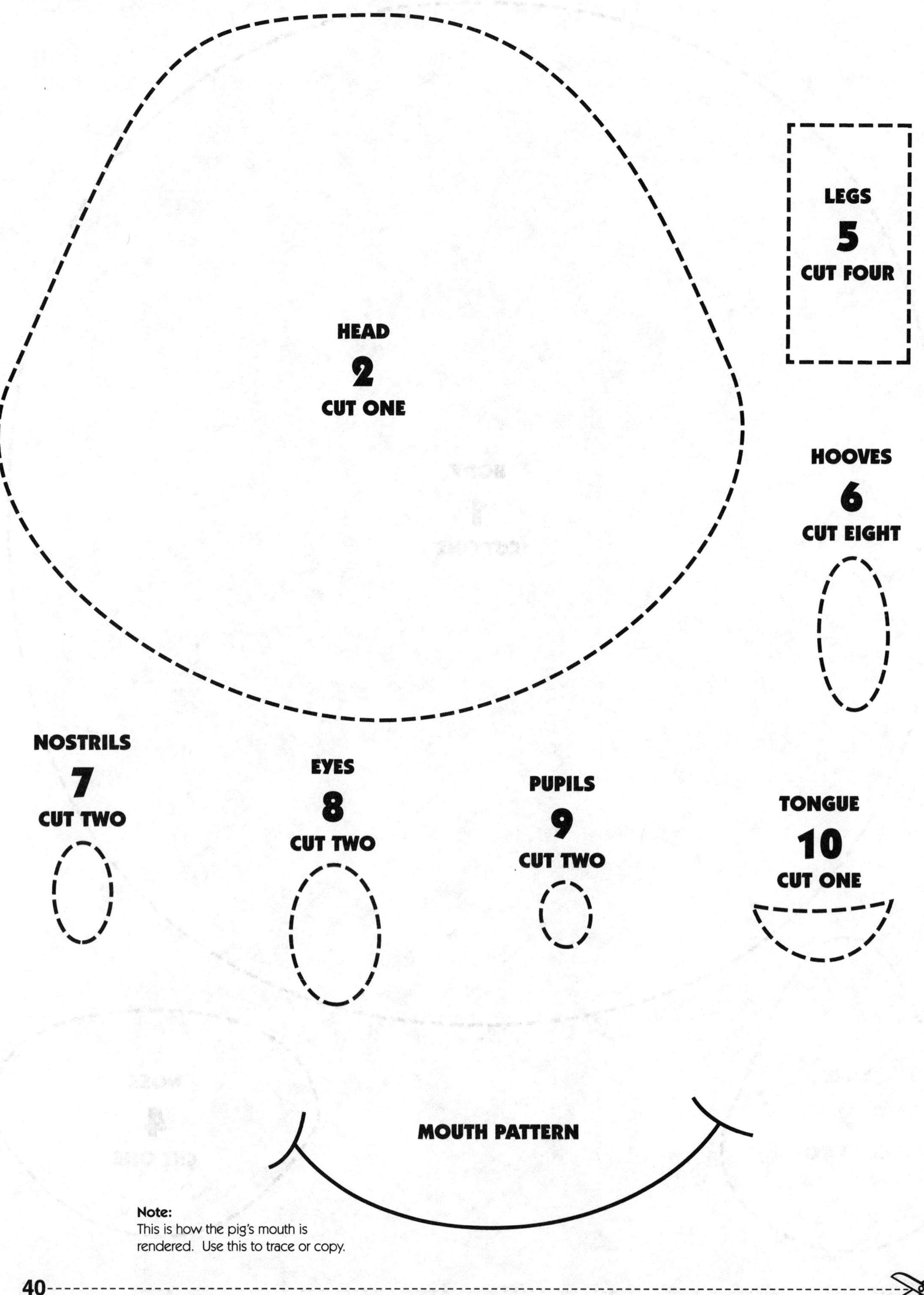

Note:
This is how the pig's mouth is rendered. Use this to trace or copy.

Materials: *black, gray, green, red and white paper; scissors; glue; black crayon or marker*

WOLF

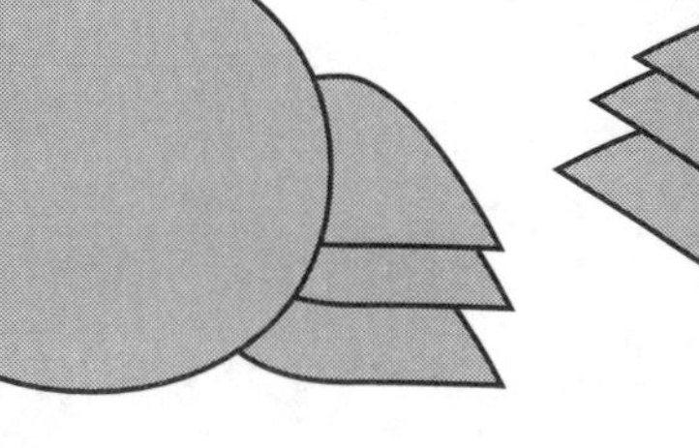

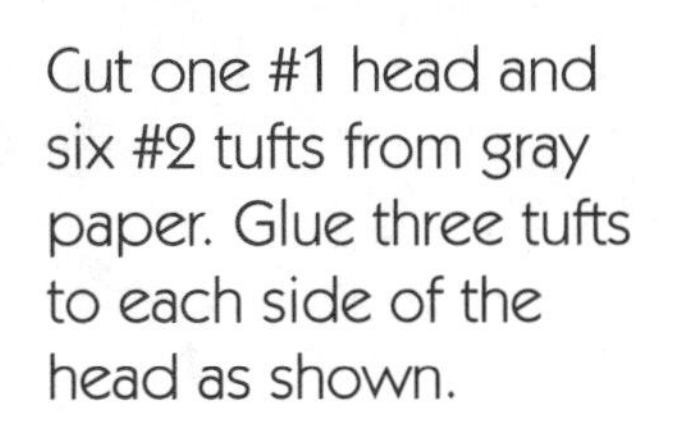

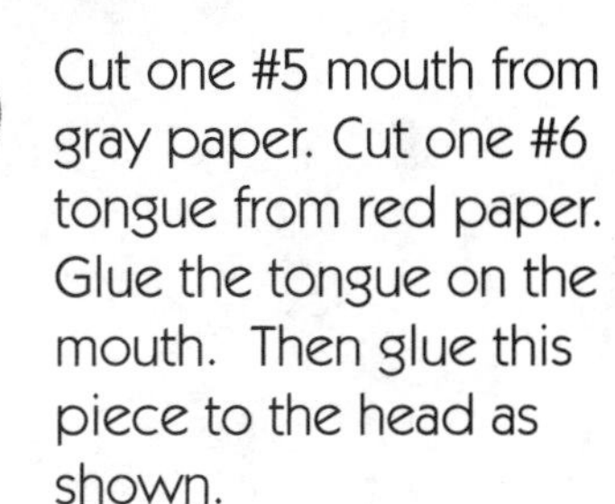

1. Cut one #1 head and six #2 tufts from gray paper. Glue three tufts to each side of the head as shown.

2. Cut two #3 ears from gray paper. Cut two #4 inner ears from white paper. Glue the inner ears on top of the #3 ears. Now glue the assembled ears to the back of the head.

3. Cut one #5 mouth from gray paper. Cut one #6 tongue from red paper. Glue the tongue on the mouth. Then glue this piece to the head as shown.

4. Cut one #7 mouth from gray paper and glue on top of the #5 mouth and tongue as shown.

5. Cut one #8 nose from black paper and glue as illustrated. Cut two #9 fangs from white paper and glue to the back of the mouth.

6. Cut two #10 eyes from white paper. Cut two #11 eyes from green paper. Cut two #12 pupils from black paper. Glue the pupils to the #11 eyes; then glue these to the #10 eyes. Now glue the assembled eyes on the head as shown. With a black crayon or marker, draw on the circles by the nose and the lines for the mouth.

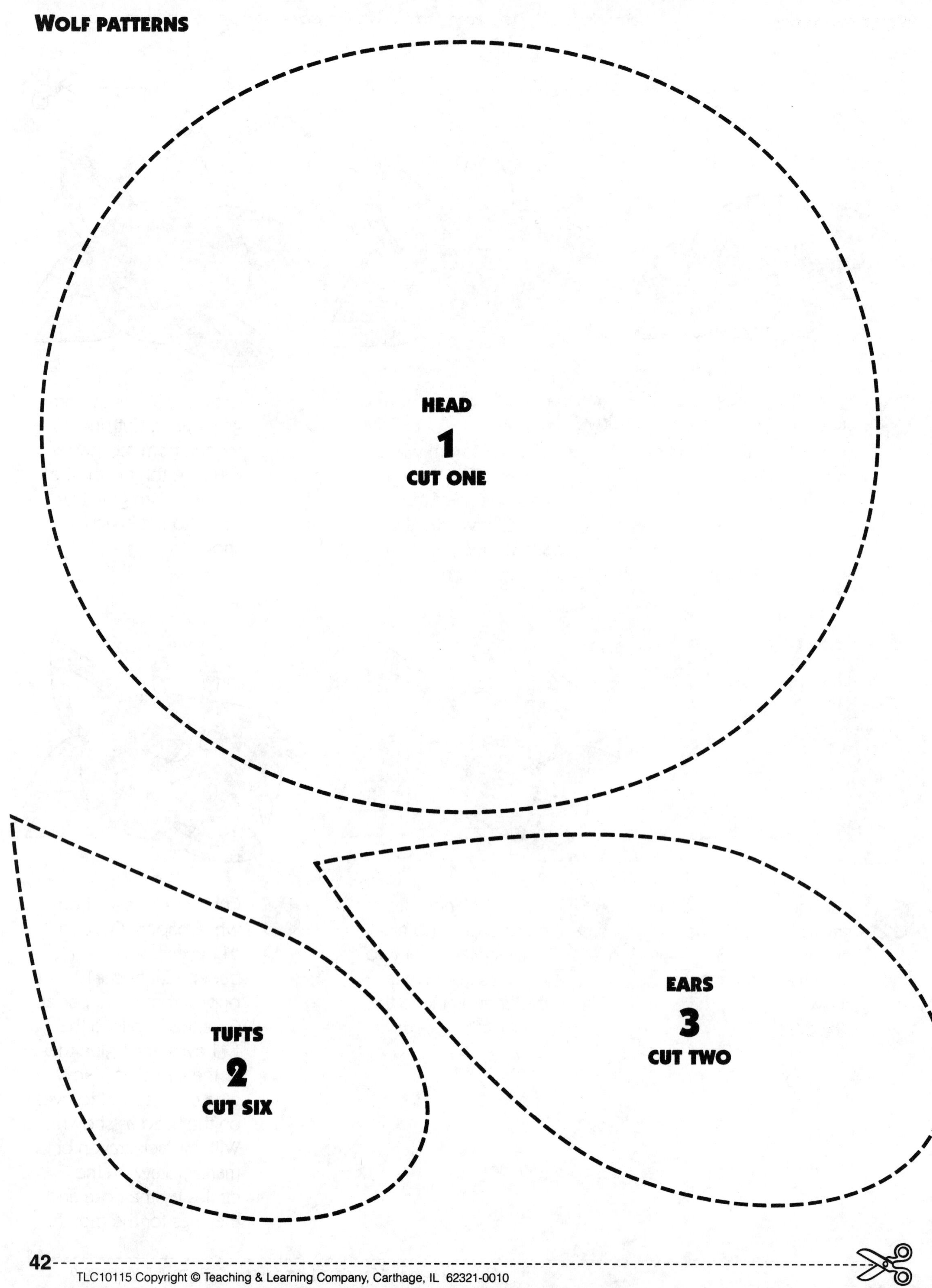
HEAD
1
CUT ONE
TUFTS
2
CUT SIX
EARS
3
CUT TWO

WOLF PATTERNS

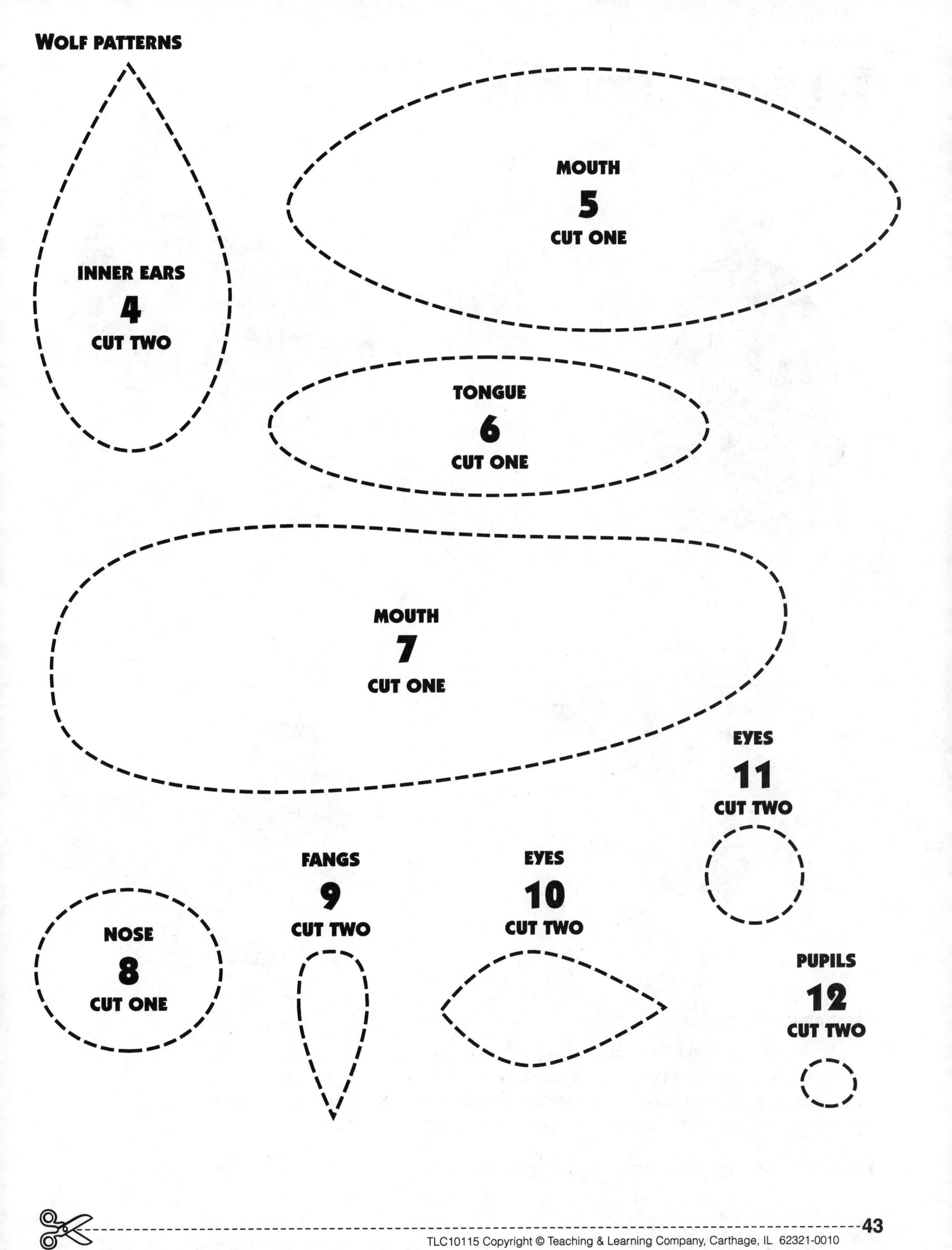

The Little Red Hen

Literature References

The Little Red Hen, retold and illustrated by Byron Barton, New York: HarperCollins, 1993.

The Little Red Hen, retold by Harriet Ziefert, illustrated by Emily Bolam, New York: Puffin Books, 1995.

The Little Red Hen, by Paul Galdone, Boston, MA: Clarion Books, 1979. Cassette available.

The Little Red Hen, by Lucinda McQueen, New York: Scholastic, 1985.

Note: Use the project on page 59 to represent the Duck.

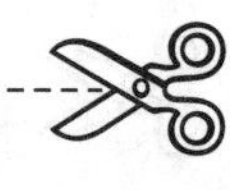

***Materials:** black, brown, red, rust, white and yellow paper; scissors; glue; black crayon or marker*
***Optional Materials:** wiggly eyes*

Little Red Hen

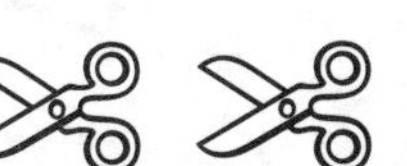

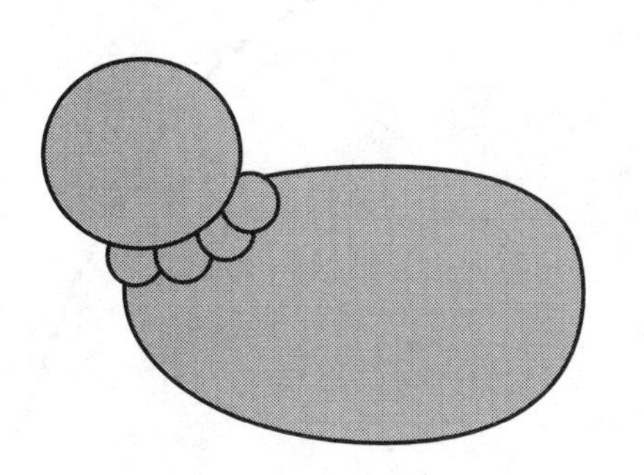

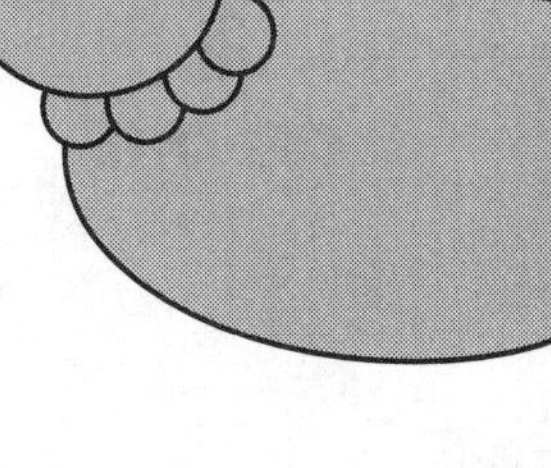

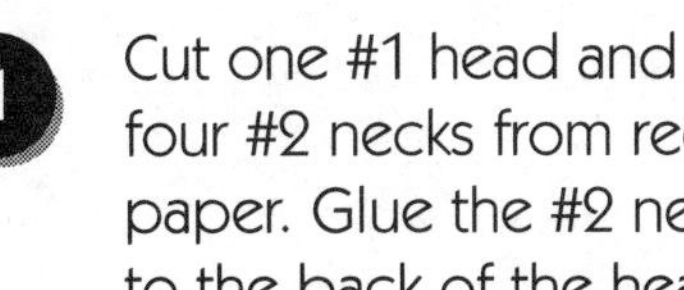

1. Cut one #1 head and four #2 necks from red paper. Glue the #2 necks to the back of the head. Cut one #3 body from red paper. Glue the headpiece to the body as shown.

2. Cut three #4 combs from rust-colored paper and glue to the back of the head as illustrated.

3. Cut three #5 tail feathers and one #6 tail feather from red paper and glue to the back of the body.

4. Cut one #7 beak from yellow paper and glue in place as shown. Cut two #8 wattles from rust-colored paper and glue to the head as shown. Cut two #9 legs from yellow paper. Glue them to the back of the body as shown. Cut two #10 feet from yellow paper. Glue one foot to the bottom of each leg. Cut four #11 toes from yellow paper and glue two to the back of each foot.

5. Cut two #12 and two #13 wings from red paper and glue as shown. Cut one #14 eye from white paper. Cut one #15 pupil from black paper. Glue the pupil on the eye. Now glue the assembled eye on the head. With a black crayon or marker, draw a line to divide the beak as shown.

Note: You may use wiggly eyes on the hen.

Little Red Hen patterns

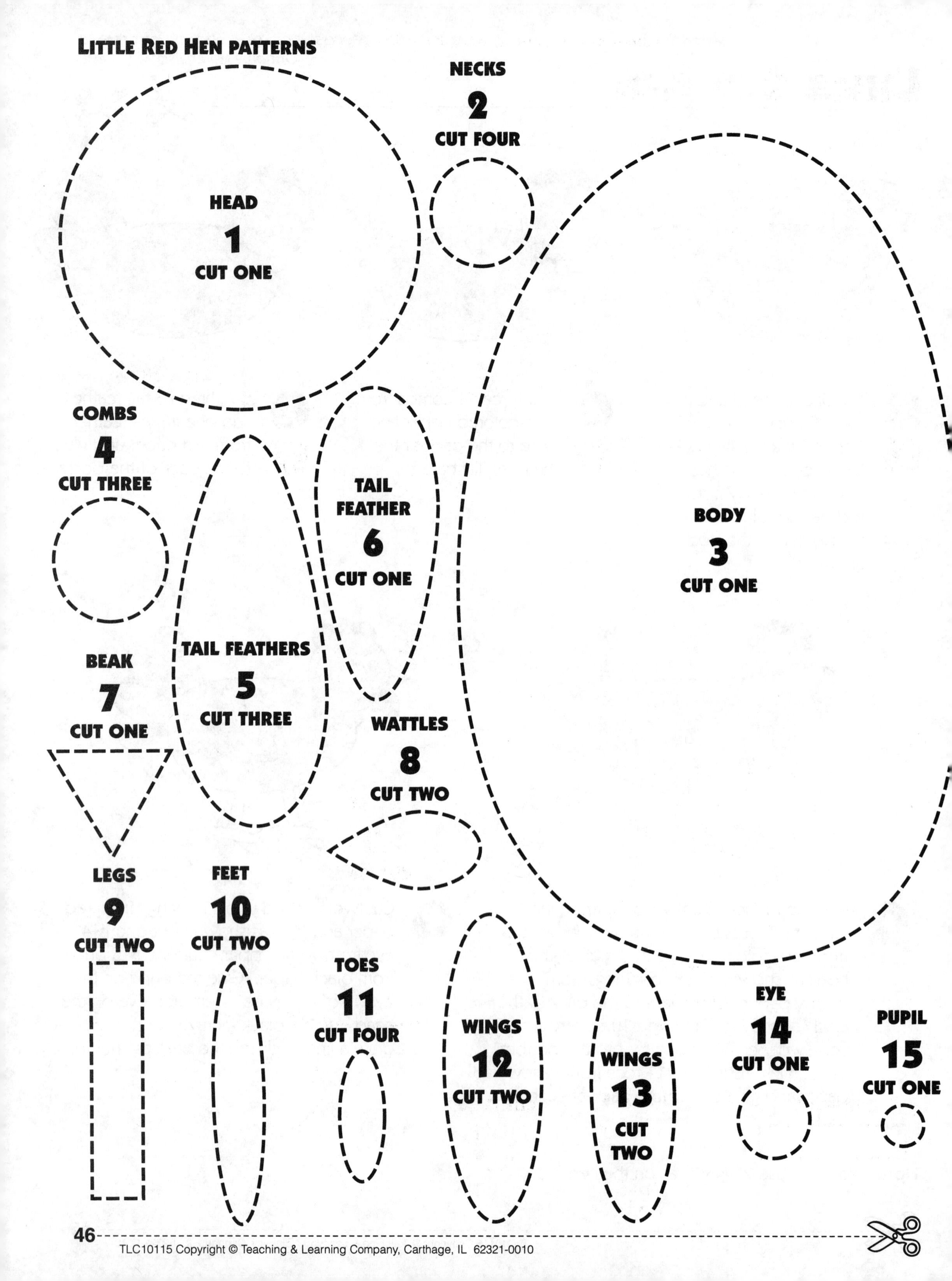

Materials: *black, orange, white and yellow paper; scissors; glue; black crayon or marker*

CHICK 1

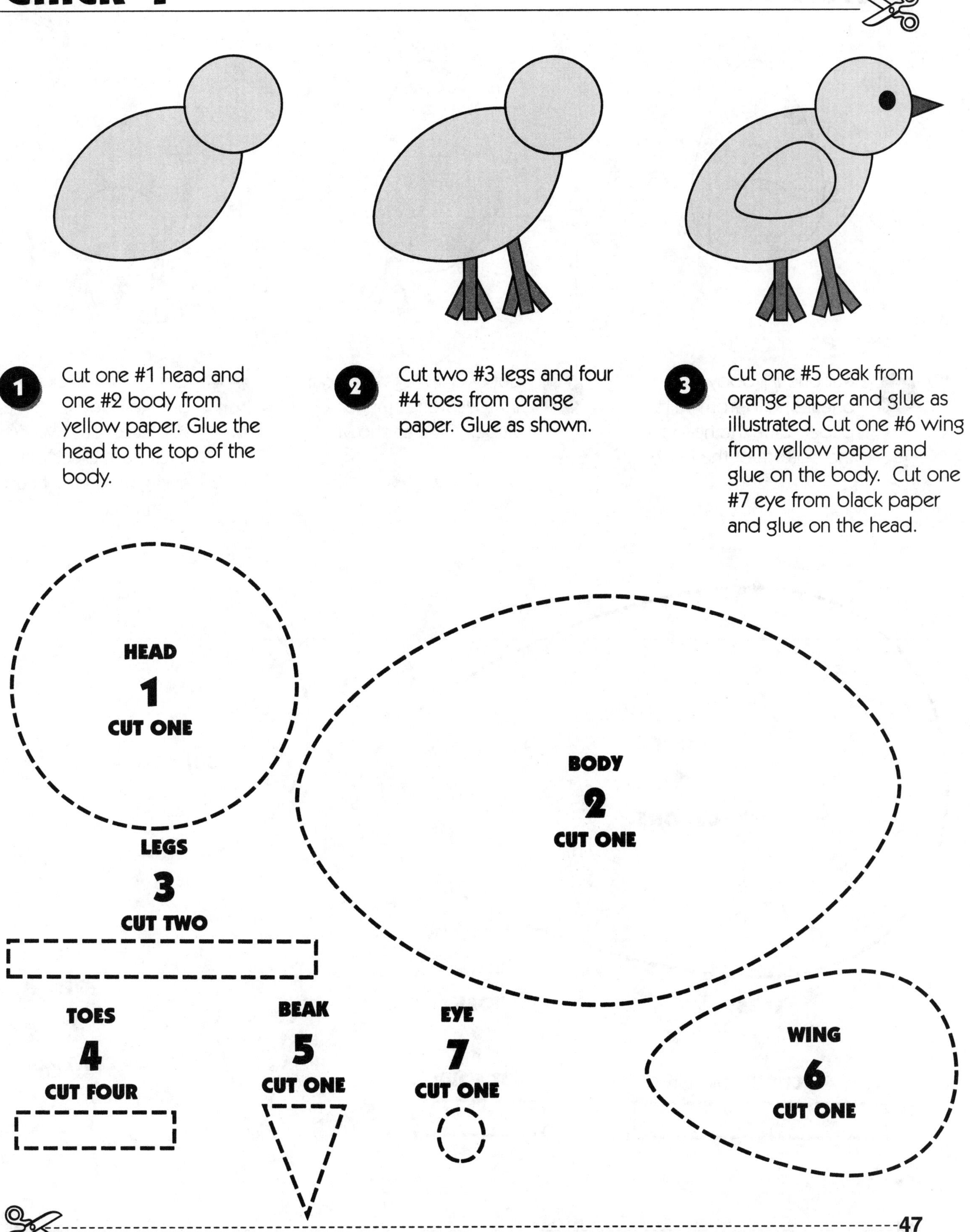

1. Cut one #1 head and one #2 body from yellow paper. Glue the head to the top of the body.
2. Cut two #3 legs and four #4 toes from orange paper. Glue as shown.
3. Cut one #5 beak from orange paper and glue as illustrated. Cut one #6 wing from yellow paper and glue on the body. Cut one #7 eye from black paper and glue on the head.

Materials: *black, orange, white and yellow paper; scissors; glue; black crayon or marker*

CHICK 2

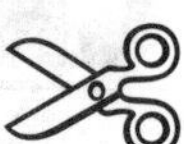

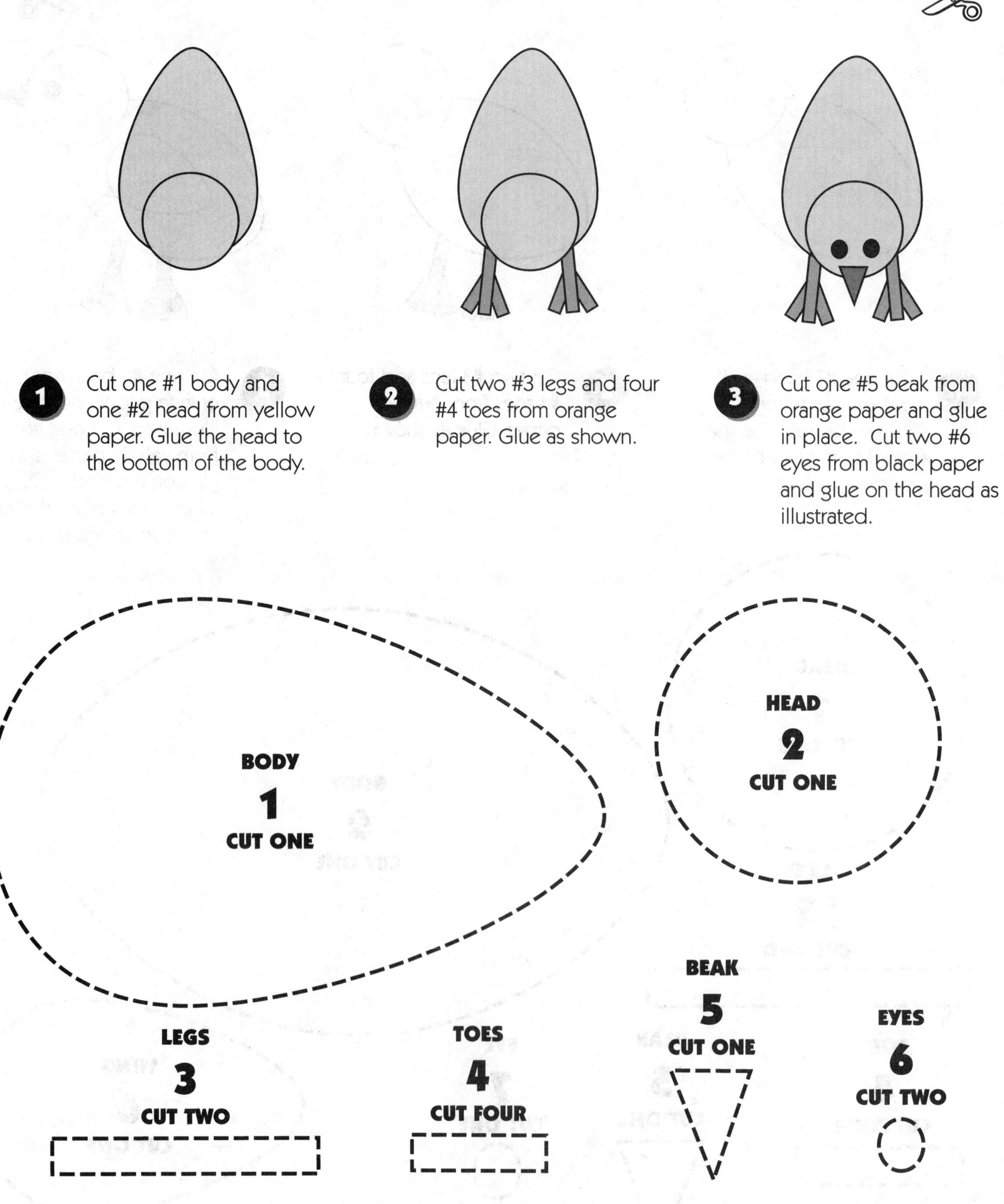

1. Cut one #1 body and one #2 head from yellow paper. Glue the head to the bottom of the body.
2. Cut two #3 legs and four #4 toes from orange paper. Glue as shown.
3. Cut one #5 beak from orange paper and glue in place. Cut two #6 eyes from black paper and glue on the head as illustrated.

Materials: *black, orange, white and yellow paper; scissors; glue; black crayon or marker*

Chick 3

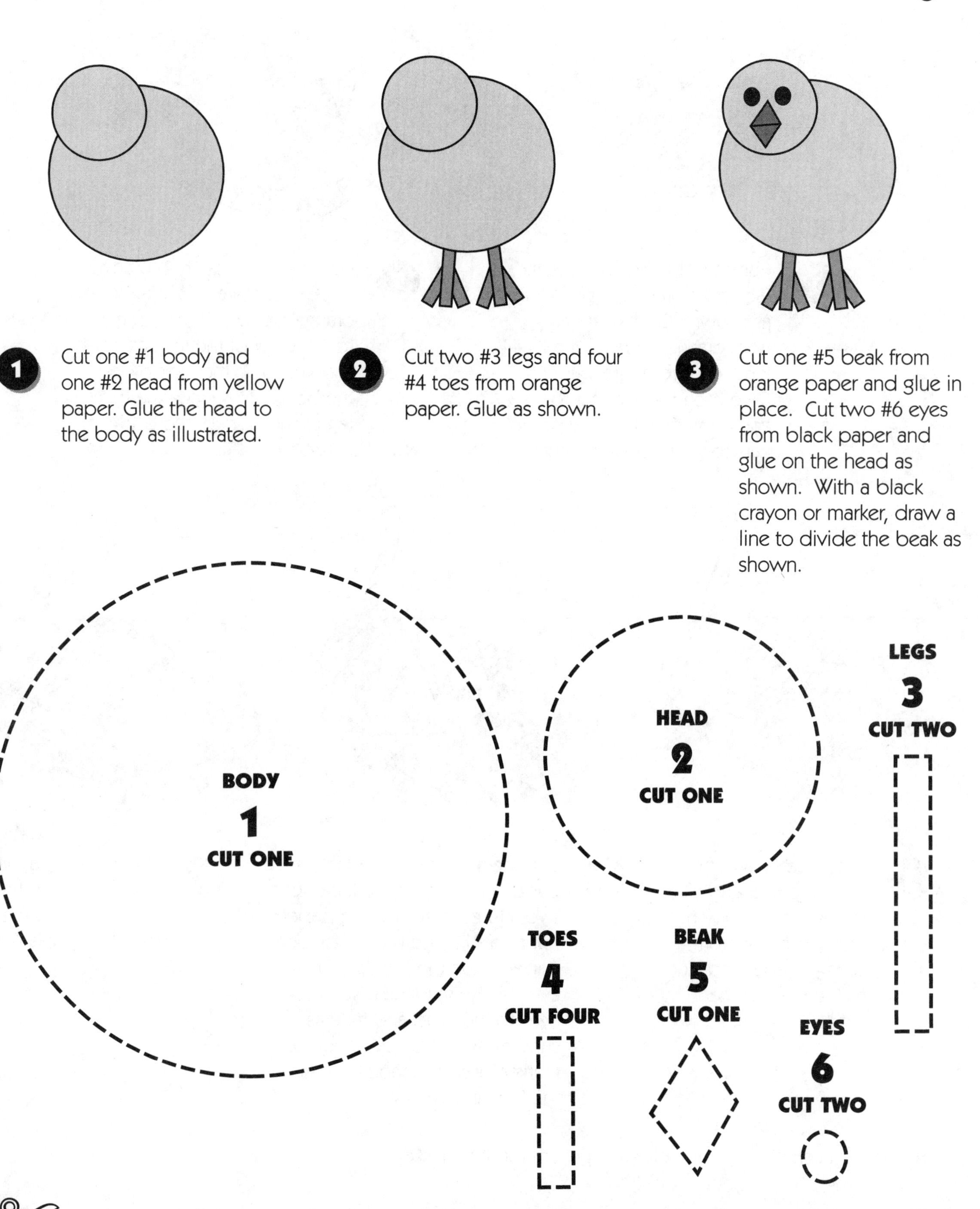

1. Cut one #1 body and one #2 head from yellow paper. Glue the head to the body as illustrated.
2. Cut two #3 legs and four #4 toes from orange paper. Glue as shown.
3. Cut one #5 beak from orange paper and glue in place. Cut two #6 eyes from black paper and glue on the head as shown. With a black crayon or marker, draw a line to divide the beak as shown.

Materials: *black, orange, pink and white paper; scissors; glue; black crayon or marker*
Optional Materials: *pipe cleaners or yarn*

CAT

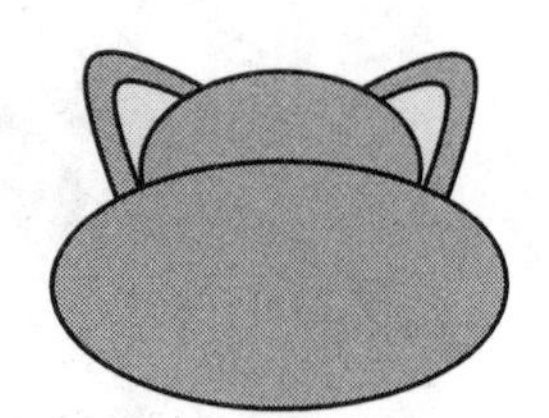

1. Cut one #1 head and one #2 face from orange paper. Glue as shown. Cut two #3 ears from orange paper. Cut two #4 inner ears from pink paper. Glue each #4 inner ear to a #3 ear. Now glue the assembled ears to the back of the head.

2. Cut one #5 body from orange paper. Cut three #6 legs from orange paper. Glue two legs to the back of the face as shown. Glue the headpiece to the body. Now glue the third leg to the back of the body as illustrated.

3. Cut three #7 feet from orange paper and glue to the legs as shown. Cut one #8 tail from orange paper and glue to the back of the body.

4. Cut one #9 nose from black paper and glue on the face. Cut two #10 eyes from white paper. Cut two #11 pupils from black paper. Glue the pupils on the eyes. Now glue the assembled eyes to the head and face as shown. With a black crayon or marker, draw the mouth, lines on the feet and whiskers.

5. Use a black crayon or marker to draw tiger-looking marks on the legs, body and tail.

Note: You can glue on pipe cleaners or yarn for the whiskers.

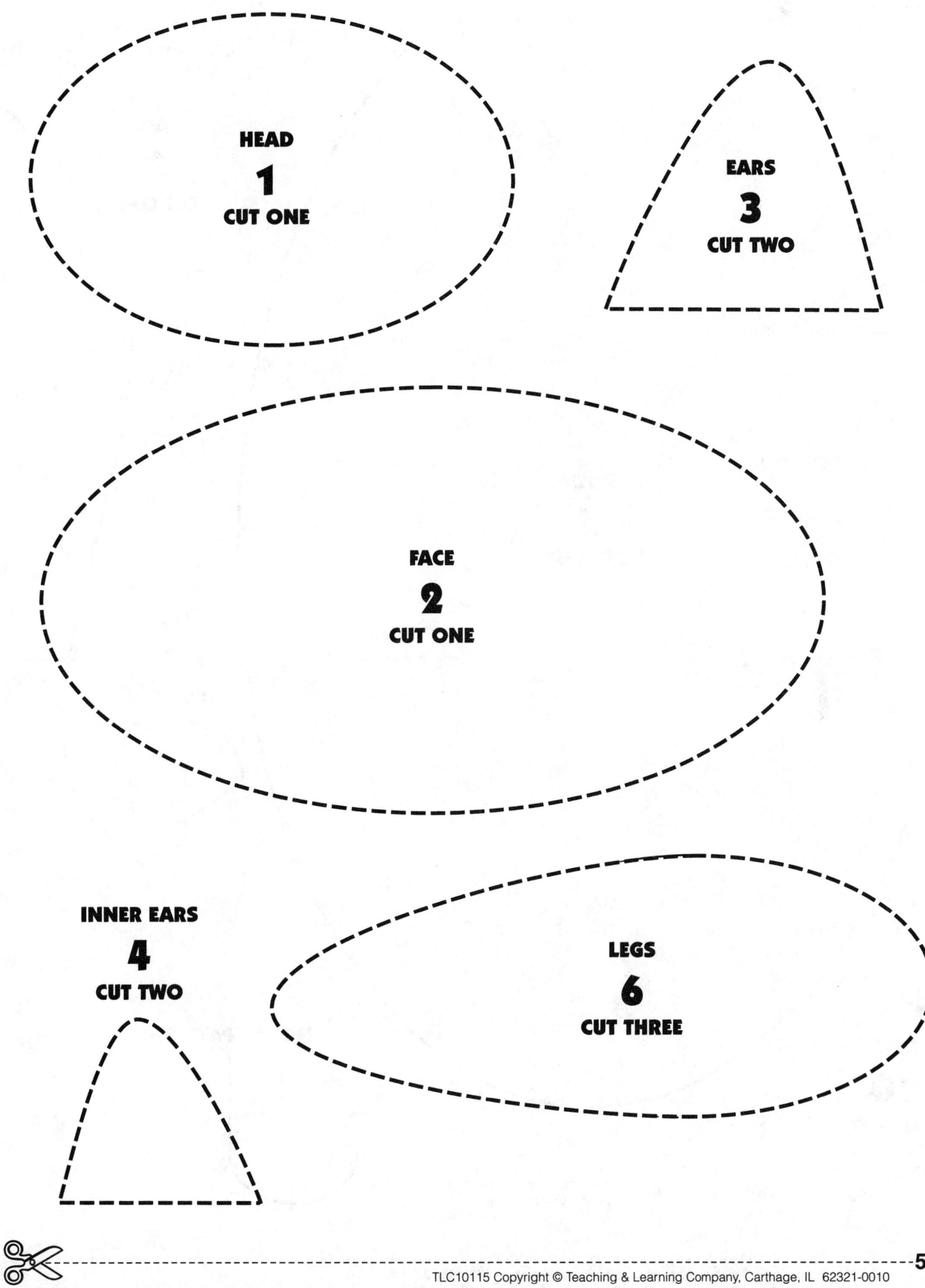
HEAD
1
CUT ONE
EARS
3
CUT TWO
FACE
2
CUT ONE
INNER EARS
4
CUT TWO
LEGS
6
CUT THREE

CAT PATTERNS

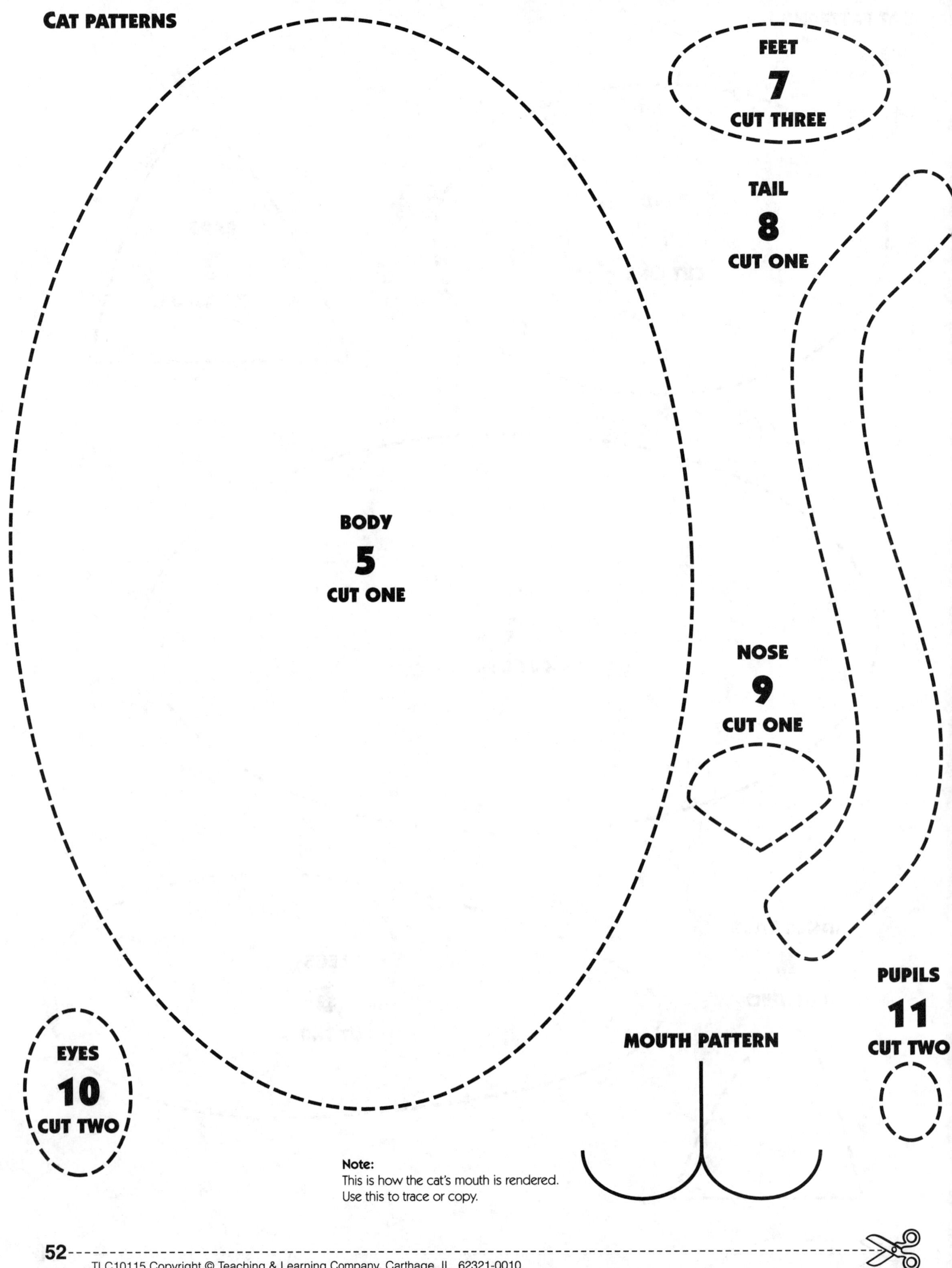

Note:
This is how the cat's mouth is rendered. Use this to trace or copy.

Materials: *black, brown and white paper; scissors; glue; black crayon or marker*

Dog

1. Cut one #1 head and one #2 face from brown paper. Glue the face on the head. Cut two #3 ears from brown paper. Glue the ears to the back of the head as shown.

2. Cut one #4 body from brown paper. Glue the headpiece to the body as shown.

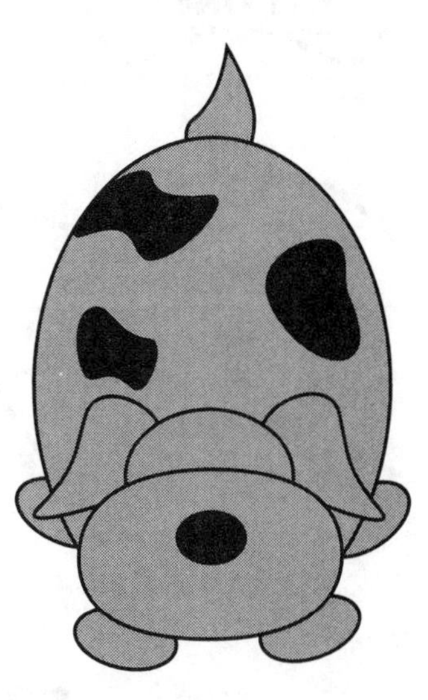

3. Cut one #5 tail from brown paper and glue to the back of the body as shown. Cut one of each of #6, #7 and #8 spots from black paper. Glue the spots as shown. Cut four #9 feet from brown paper and glue to the face and body as illustrated. Cut one #10 nose from black paper. Glue the nose on the face.

4. Cut two #11 eyes from white paper. Cut two #12 pupils from black paper. Glue the pupils on the eyes as shown. Cut two #13 eyelids from tan paper and glue on the eyes. Now glue the assembled eyes on the head and face as illustrated.

5. Cut one #14 tongue from red paper and glue in place as shown. With a black crayon or marker, draw on the whiskers, mouth and lines on the feet.

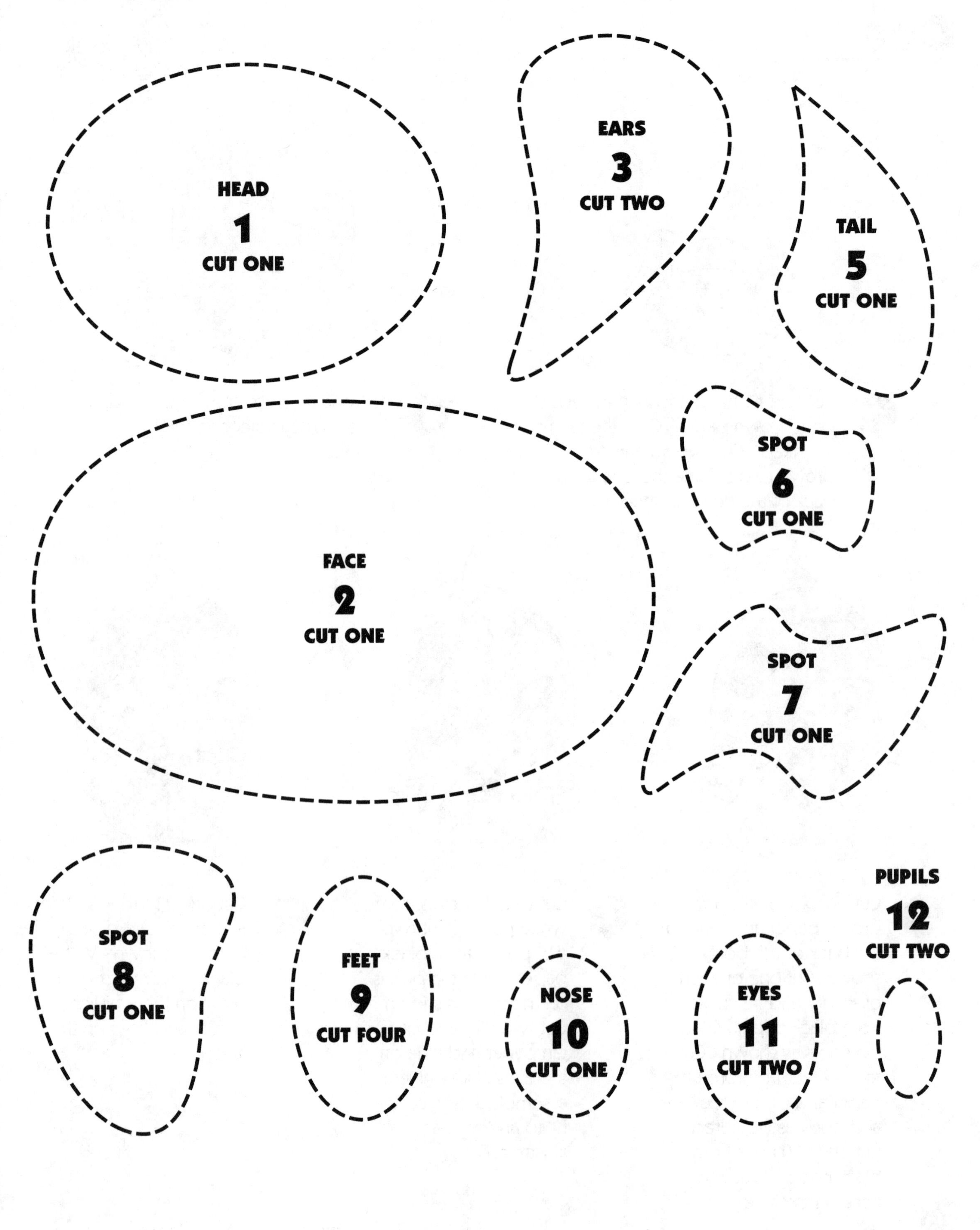
HEAD
1
CUT ONE
EARS
3
CUT TWO
TAIL
5
CUT ONE
SPOT
6
CUT ONE
FACE
2
CUT ONE
SPOT
7
CUT ONE
SPOT
8
CUT ONE
FEET
9
CUT FOUR
NOSE
10
CUT ONE
EYES
11
CUT TWO
PUPILS
12
CUT TWO

Dog patterns

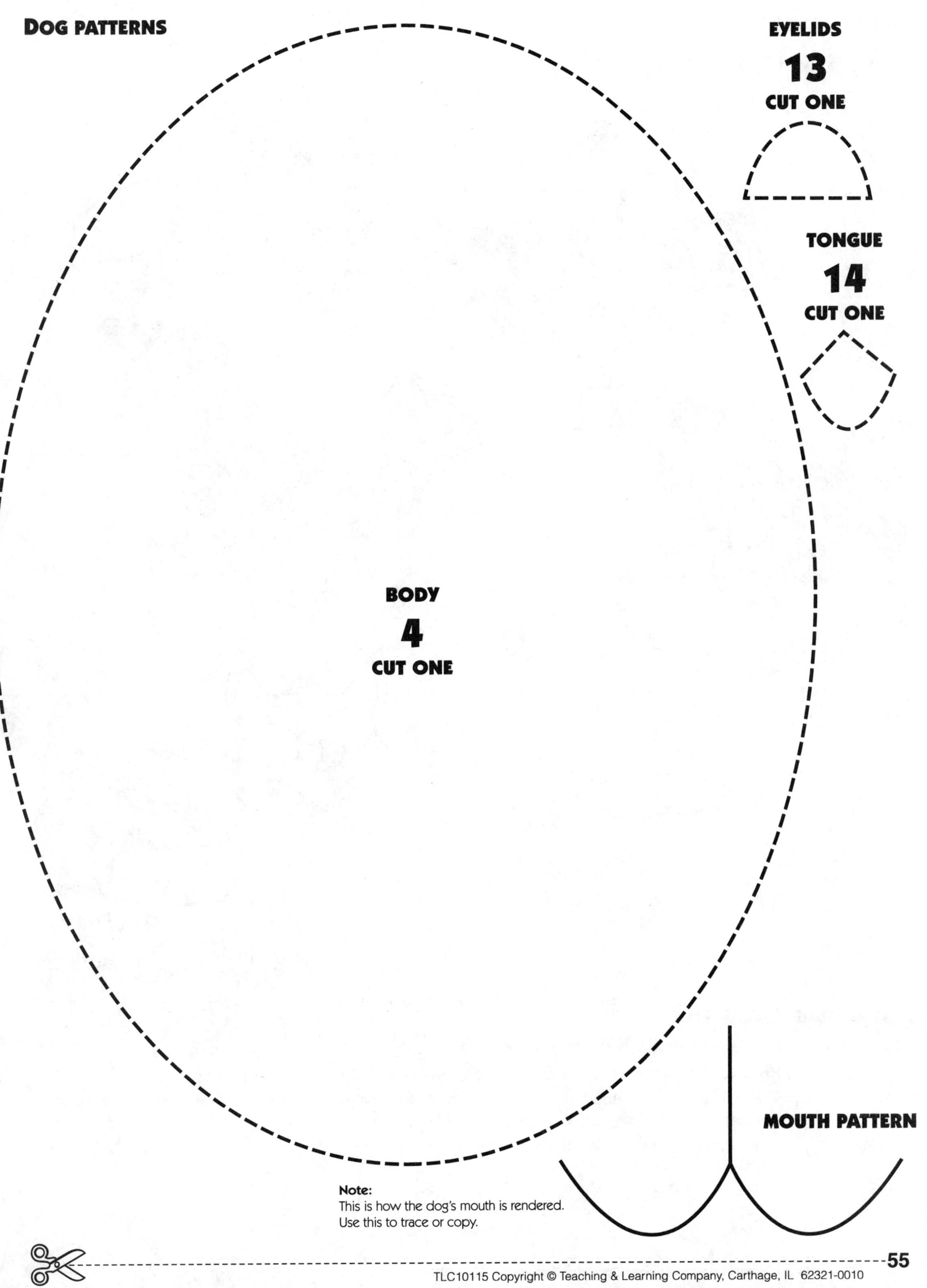

Note:
This is how the dog's mouth is rendered.
Use this to trace or copy.

Henny Penny

Literature References

Henny Penny, by Paul Galdone, Boston, MA: Clarion Books, 1979.

Henny Penny, by Harriet Ziefert, illustrated by Emily Bolam, New York: Puffin Books.

Henny Penny/Brainy Bird Saves the Day! (Another Point of View), by Alvin Granowsky, illustrated by Eva Vagretti Cockrille and Mike Krone, New York: Raintree/Steck-Vaughn (paperback), 1996.

Henny Penny, by H. Werner Zimmerman, New York: Scholastic, 1989.

Note: Use the project on page 45 to represent Henny Penny.

Materials: *black, brown, orange, red, tan, white and yellow paper; scissors; glue; black crayon or marker*
Optional Materials: *wiggly eyes*

Cocky Locky

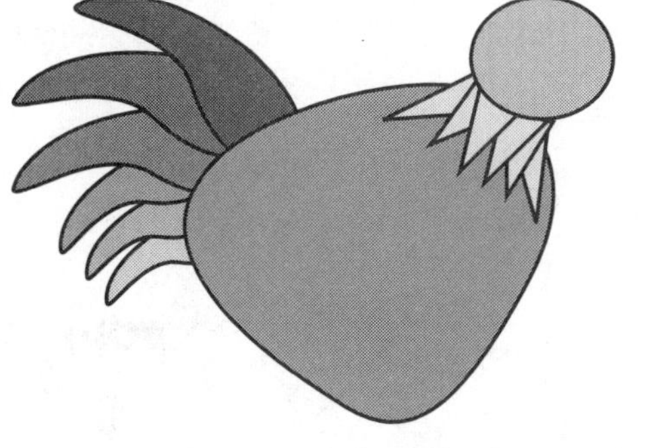

1 Cut one #1 body from brown paper.

Cut three #2 tail feathers one each from brown, red and orange paper and glue to the back of the body as shown.

3 Cut two #3 tail feathers one each from brown and orange paper and glue in place as shown. Cut one #4 tail feather from red paper and glue to the back of the body. Cut one #5 head from brown paper. Cut three #6 and three #7 neck feathers from tan paper and glue to the back of the head as illustrated. Then glue the assembled head to the body.

Cut four #8 combs from red paper and glue to the top of the head. Cut one #9 wing from brown paper. Glue the wing on the body as shown.

Cut two #10 legs and two #11 feet from orange paper. Glue one foot to the bottom of each leg. Cut four #12 toes from orange paper and glue two to the back of each leg.

6 Cut one #13 beak from yellow paper and glue to the back of the head. Cut two #14 wattles from red paper and glue to the head as shown. Cut one #15 eye from white paper. Cut one #16 pupil from black paper. Glue the pupil on the eye as shown. Now glue the assembled eye on the head. With a black crayon or marker, draw the line to divide the beak.

Note: You may use wiggly eyes on Cocky Locky.

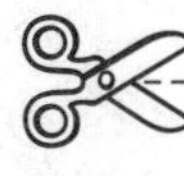

Cocky Locky patterns

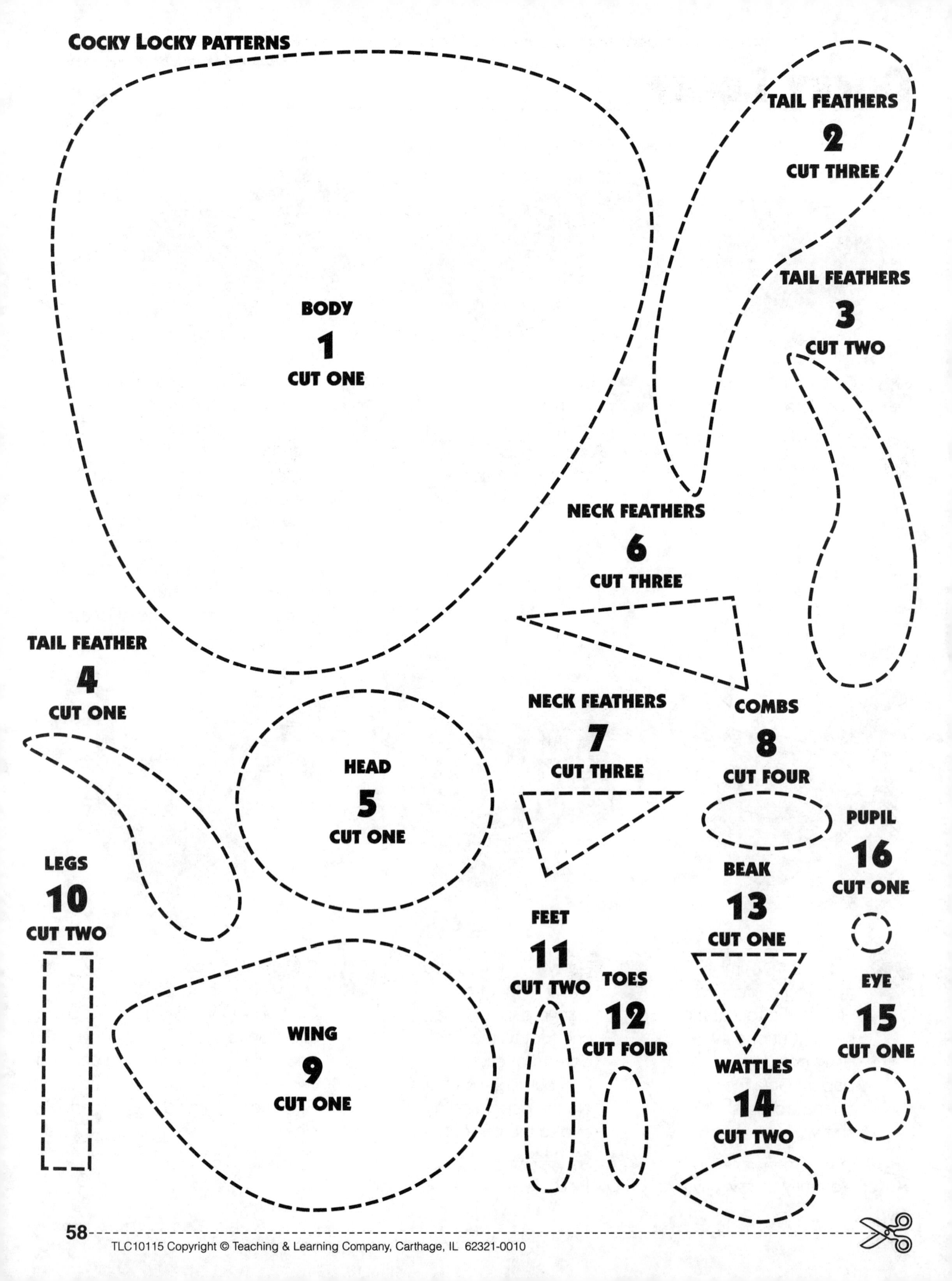

Materials: *black, orange, white and yellow paper; scissors; glue; black crayon or marker*
Optional Materials: *wiggly eyes*

Ducky Lucky

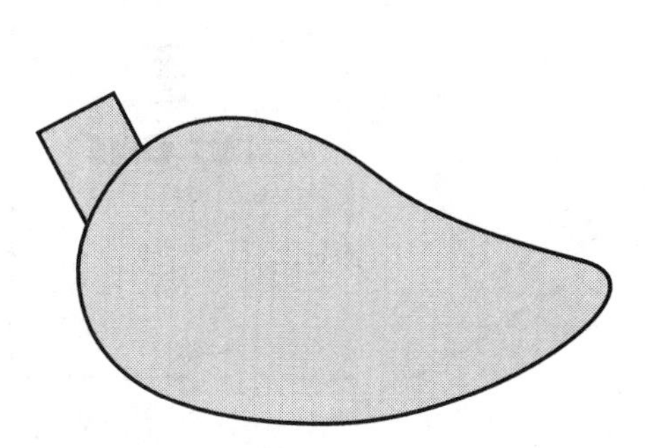

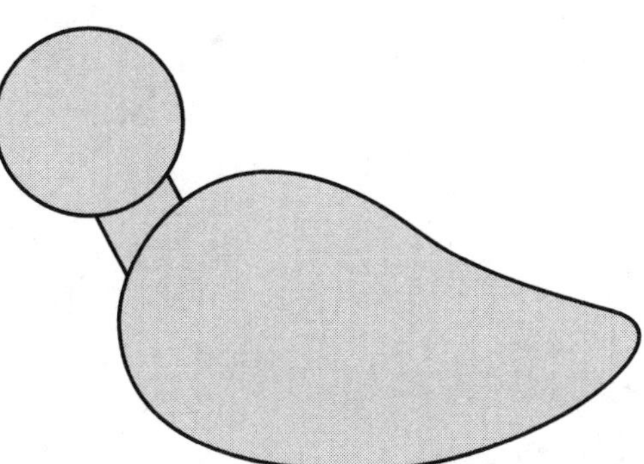

1 Cut one #1 body and one #2 neck from yellow paper. Glue the neck to the back of the body.

2 Cut one #3 head from yellow paper and glue to the top of the neck.

3 Cut two #4 legs from orange paper and glue to the body as shown. Cut two #5 feet from orange paper. Glue one foot to the bottom of each leg.

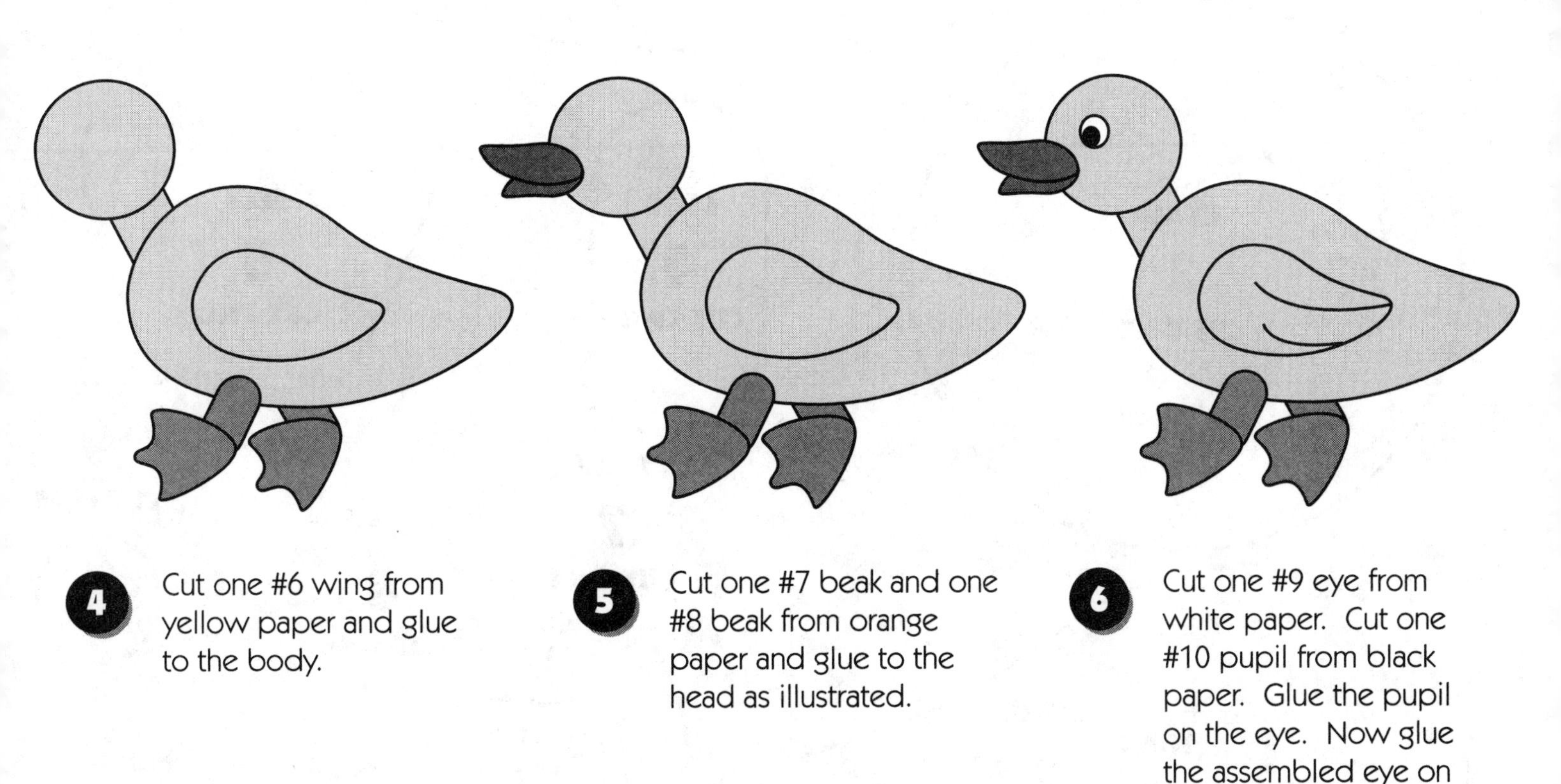

4 Cut one #6 wing from yellow paper and glue to the body.

5 Cut one #7 beak and one #8 beak from orange paper and glue to the head as illustrated.

6 Cut one #9 eye from white paper. Cut one #10 pupil from black paper. Glue the pupil on the eye. Now glue the assembled eye on the head. With a black crayon or marker, draw the lines on the wing as illustrated.

Note: You may use wiggly eyes for Ducky Lucky.

DUCKY LUCKY PATTERNS

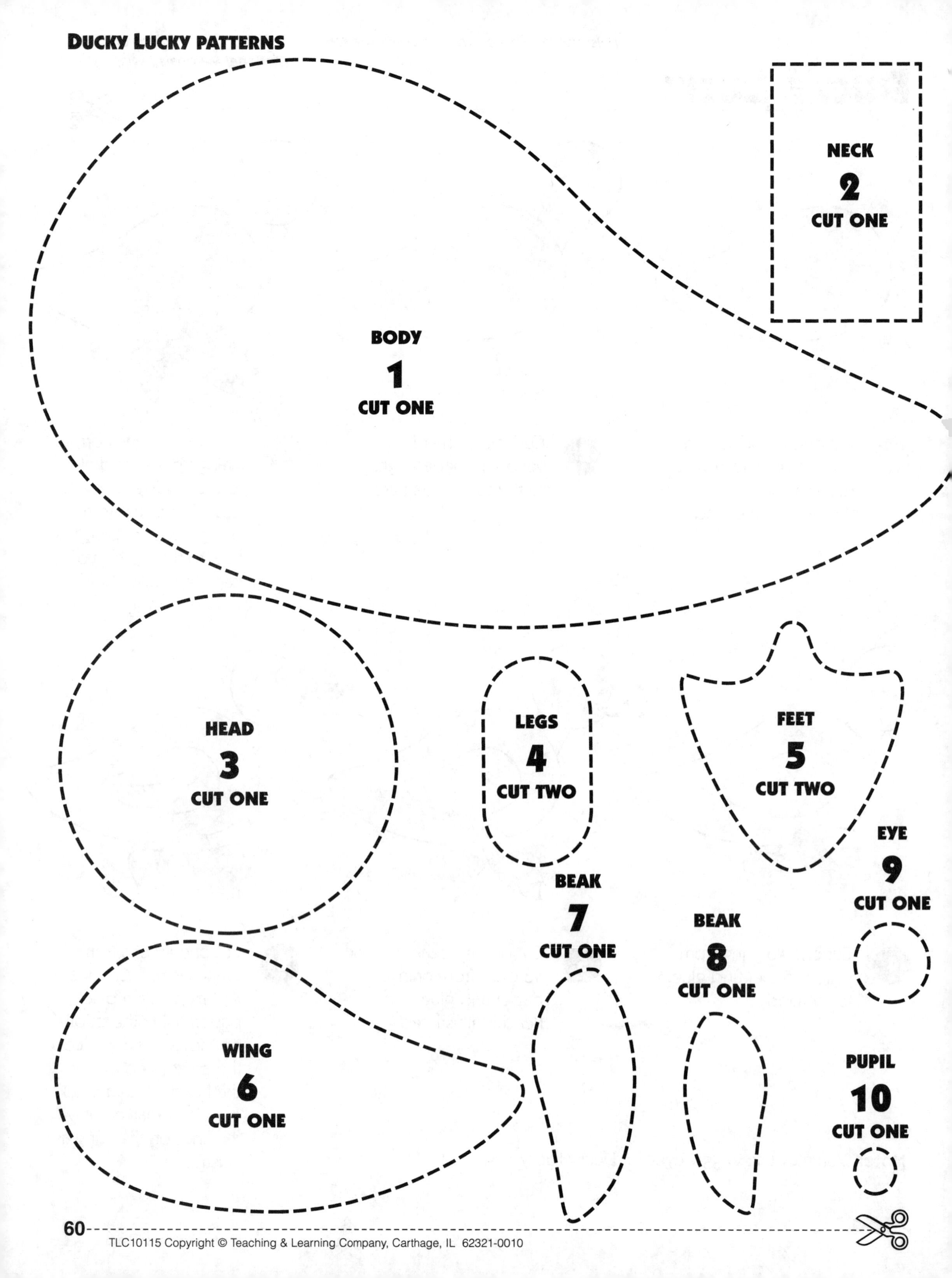

Materials: *black, red, rust and white paper; scissors; glue; black crayon or marker*
Optional Materials: *wiggly eyes*

Foxy Loxy

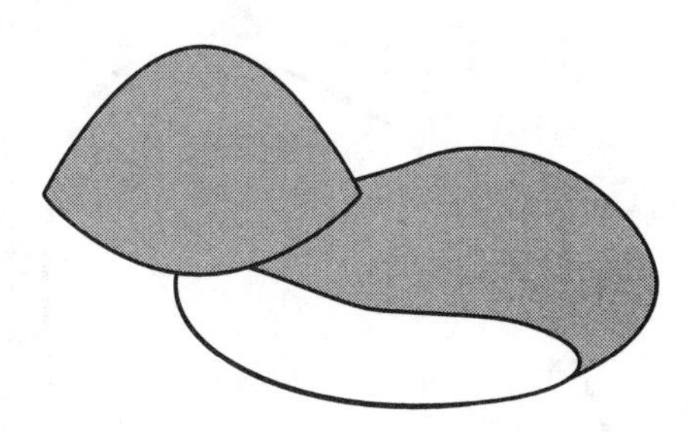

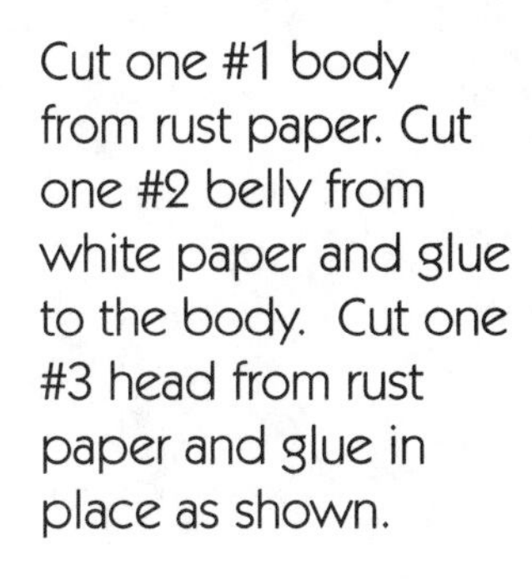

1 Cut one #1 body from rust paper. Cut one #2 belly from white paper and glue to the body. Cut one #3 head from rust paper and glue in place as shown.

2 Cut two #4 ears from rust paper and two #5 inner ears from white paper. Glue the inner ears on the #4 ears. Then glue the assembled ears to the back of the head as shown. Cut two #6 tails, one from rust paper and one from white paper. Glue the white tail to the back of the rust-colored tail and then glue to the back of the body as illustrated.

3 Cut one #7 hip from rust paper and glue at the back of the body. Cut one #8 mouth from white paper and glue in place. Cut one #9 tongue from red paper and glue to the #8 mouth.

4 Cut one #10 mouth from rust paper and glue to top of mouth as shown. Cut four #11 legs from rust paper and glue as shown. Cut four #12 feet from rust paper. Glue one foot to the bottom of each leg.

Note: You may use wiggly eyes for Foxy Loxy.

5 Cut one #13 nose from black paper and glue to the mouth as shown. Cut several of the provided hair patterns from rust paper and glue to the top of the head to make a forelock. Cut two #14 eyes from white paper. Cut two #15 pupils from black paper. Glue the pupils on the eyes. Now glue the assembled eyes to the head as shown. With a black crayon or marker, draw the lines on the feet as illustrated.

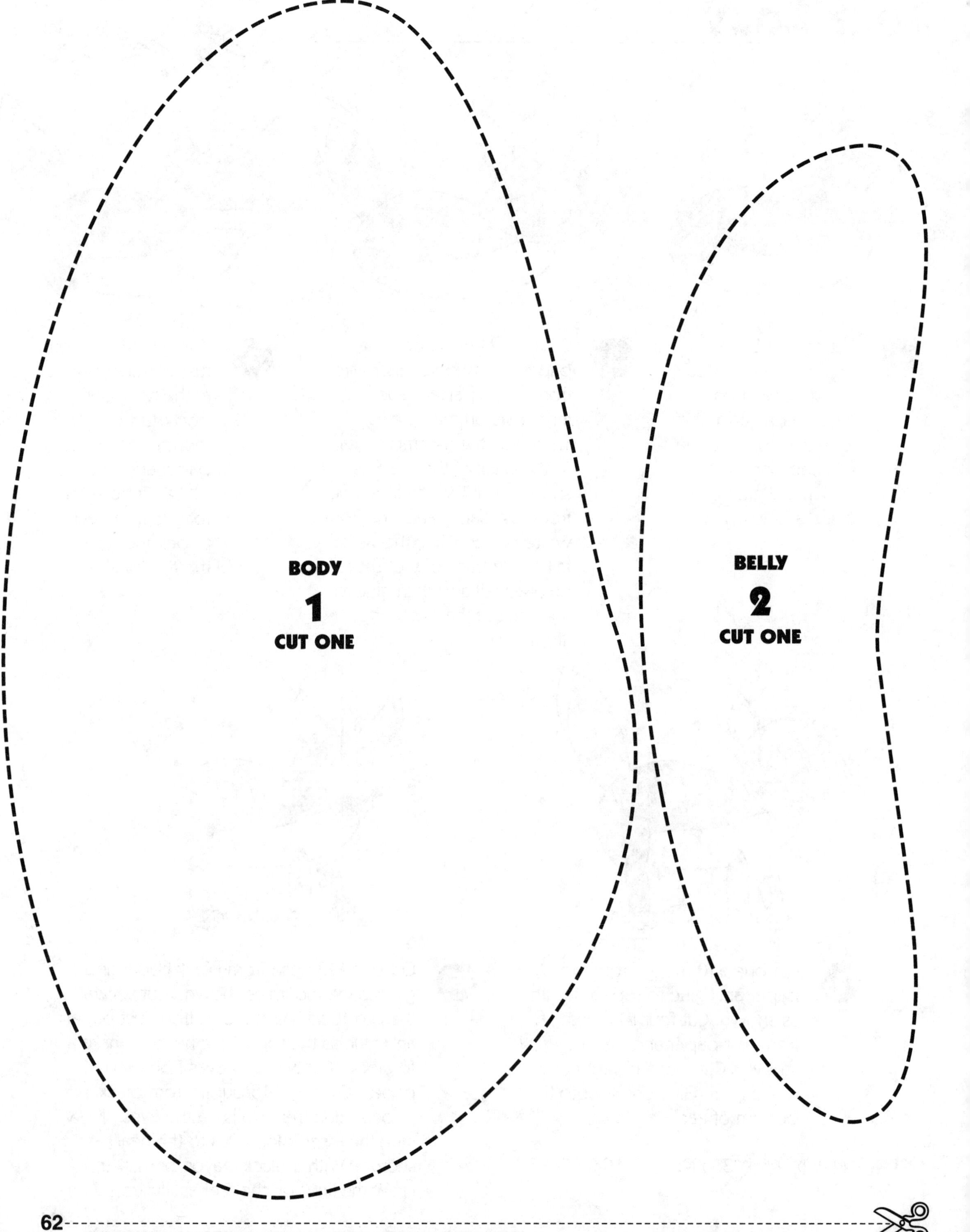
BODY
1
CUT ONE
BELLY
2
CUT ONE

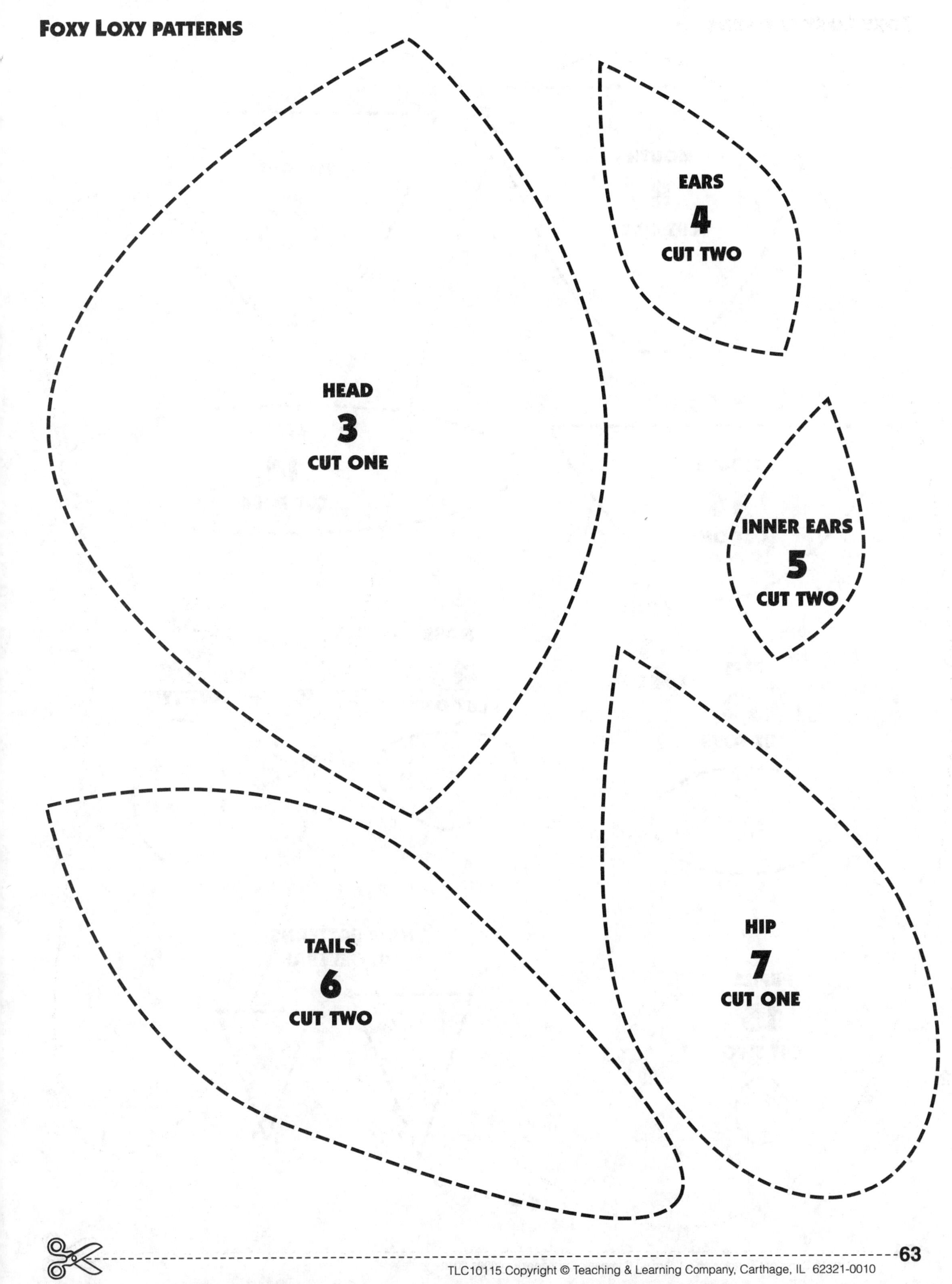
EARS
4
CUT TWO
HEAD
3
CUT ONE
INNER EARS
5
CUT TWO
TAILS
6
CUT TWO
HIP
7
CUT ONE

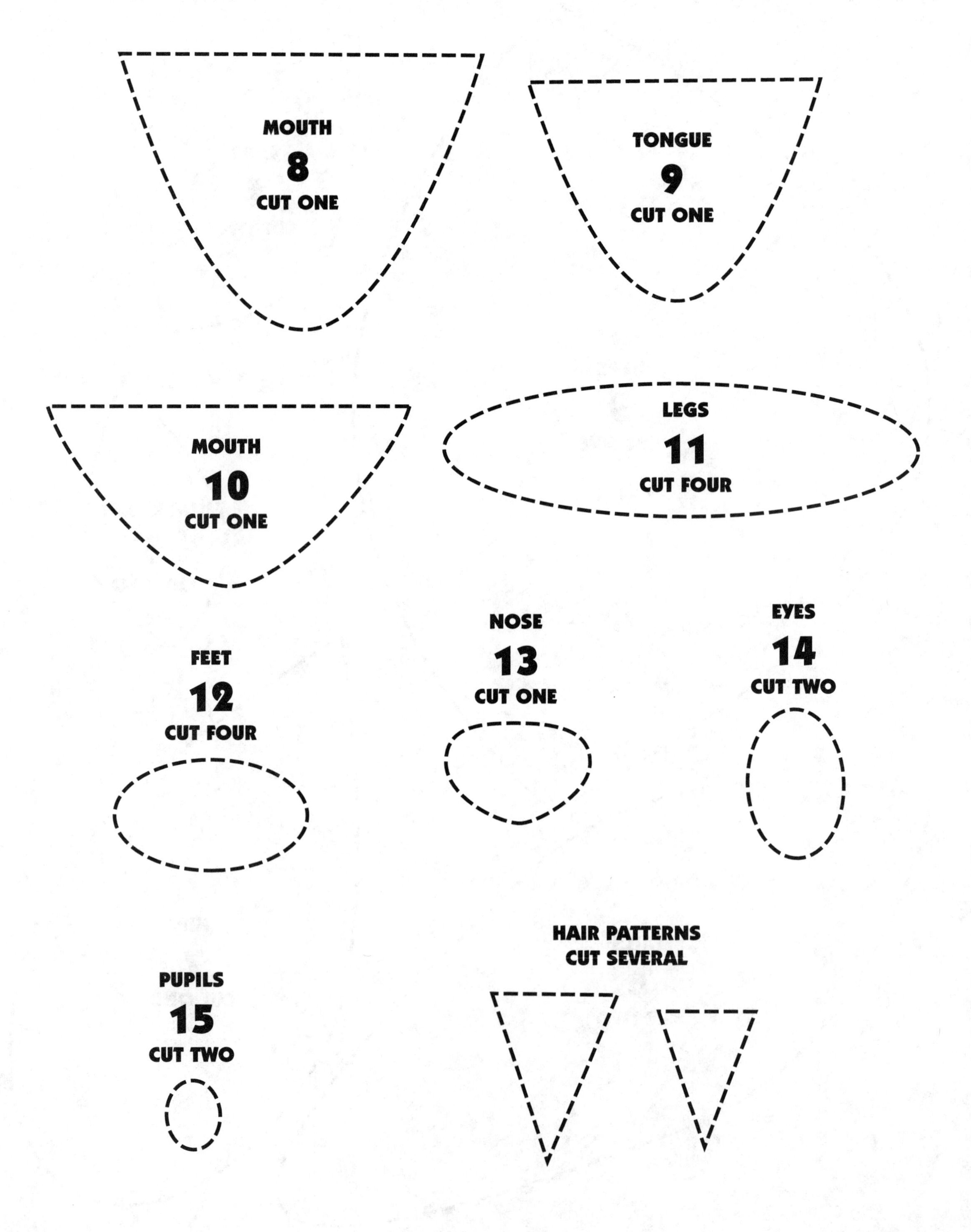
MOUTH
8
CUT ONE
TONGUE
9
CUT ONE
MOUTH
10
CUT ONE
LEGS
11
CUT FOUR
FEET
12
CUT FOUR
NOSE
13
CUT ONE
EYES
14
CUT TWO
PUPILS
15
CUT TWO
HAIR PATTERNS
CUT SEVERAL

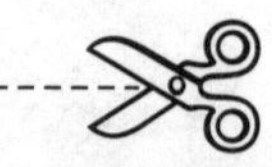

Materials: *black, orange and white paper; scissors; glue; black crayon or marker*

Goosey Loosey

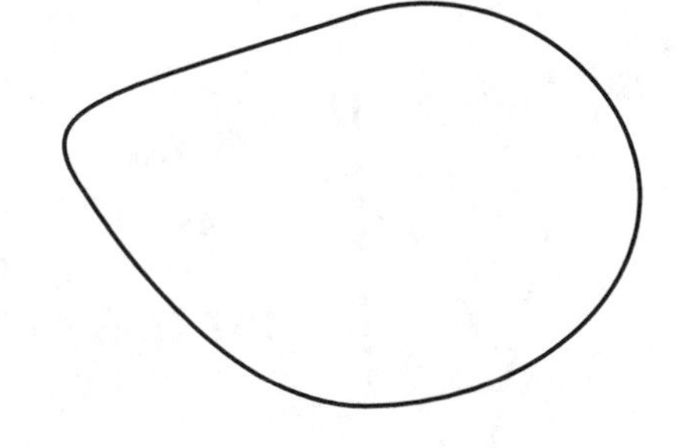

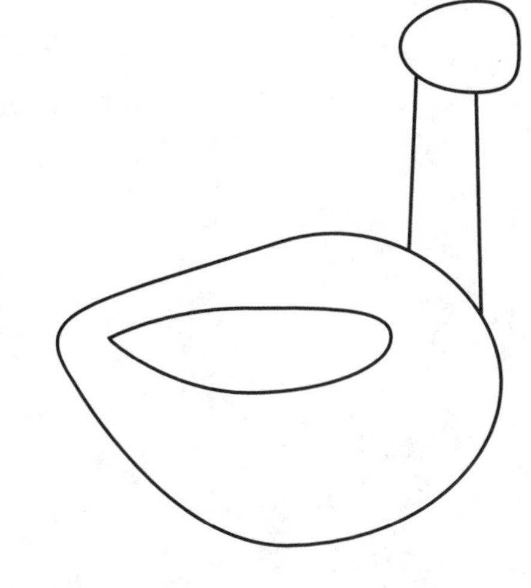

1 Cut one #1 body from white paper.

Cut one #2 neck and one #3 head from white paper and glue as shown.

Cut one #4 wing from white paper and glue on the body.

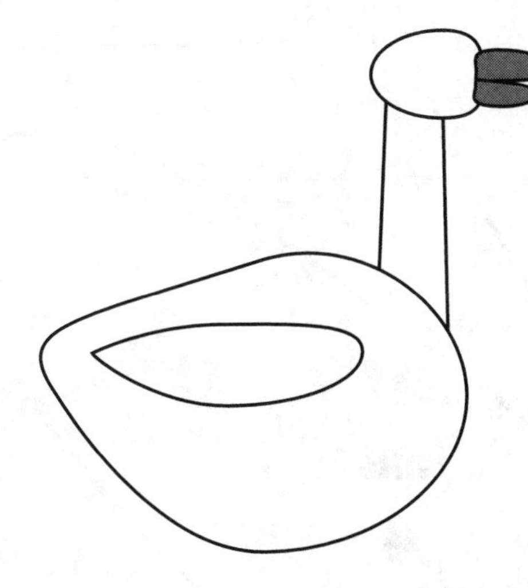

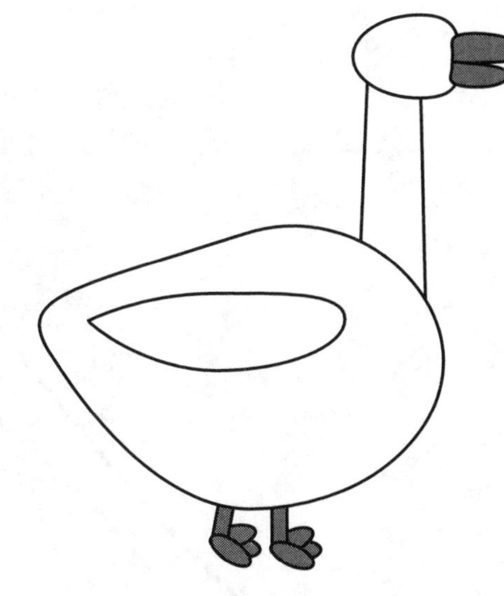

4 Cut one #5 beak and one #6 beak from orange paper and glue to the head as illustrated.

Cut two #7 legs from orange paper and glue to the back of the body. Cut six #8 toes from orange paper. Glue three toes to the bottom of each leg as shown.

With a black crayon or marker, draw on an eye.

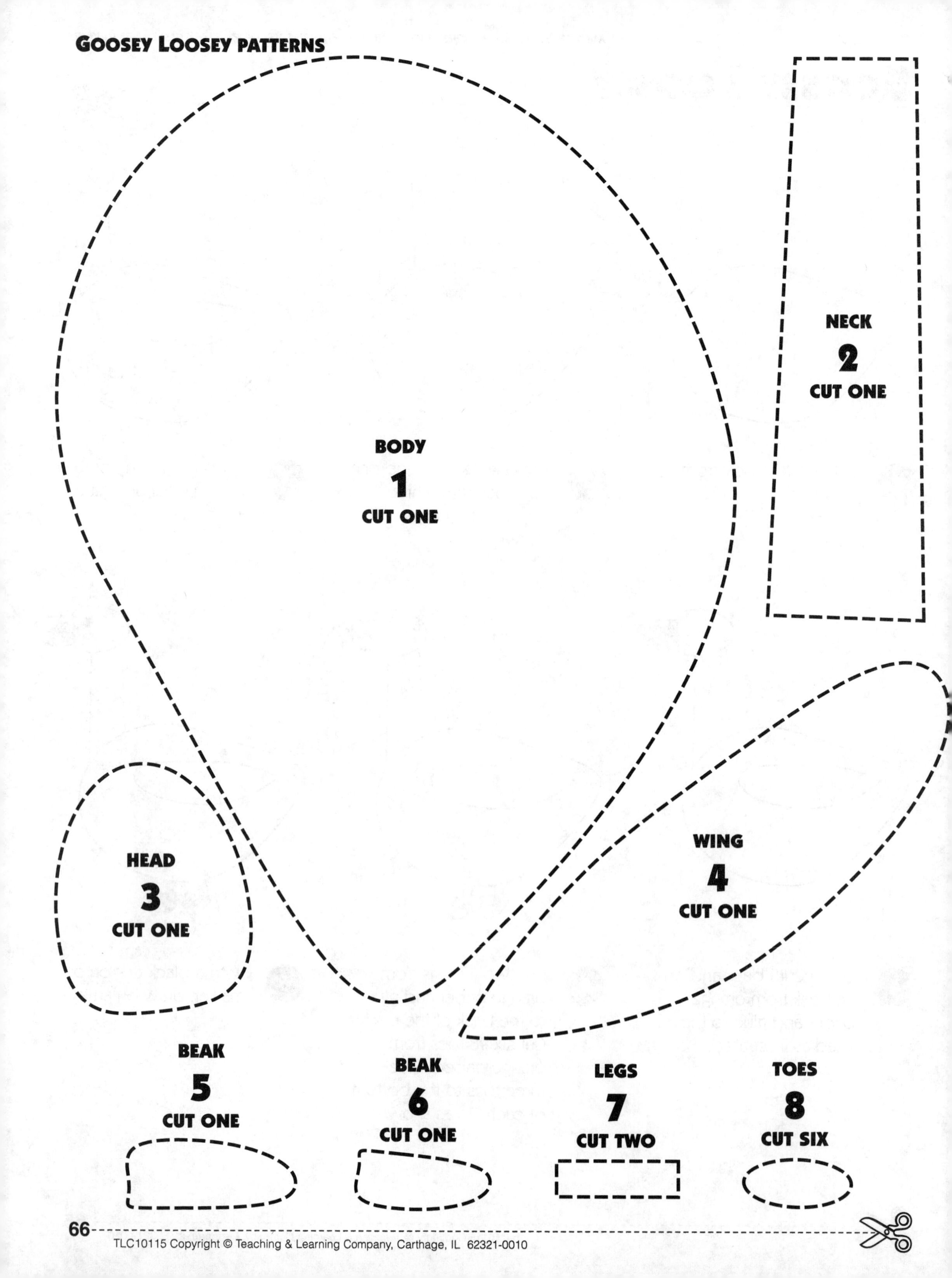
BODY
1
CUT ONE
NECK
2
CUT ONE
HEAD
3
CUT ONE
WING
4
CUT ONE
BEAK
5
CUT ONE
BEAK
6
CUT ONE
LEGS
7
CUT TWO
TOES
8
CUT SIX

Materials: *black, brown, orange, red, tan, white and yellow paper; scissors; glue; black crayon or marker*

TURKEY LURKEY

Cut one #1 body from tan paper. Cut seven #2 feathers from red, orange, yellow and brown paper. Glue the feathers to the back of the body. Cut two #3 feathers from tan paper and glue to the side of the body as shown.

2 Cut one #4 neck from tan paper and glue at the top of the body as illustrated.

Cut one #5 head from tan paper and glue at the top of the neck.

Cut two #6 wings from tan paper and glue in place as shown. Cut one #7 and one #8 beak from orange paper and glue at the side of the head as shown.

5 Cut two #9 wattles from red paper and glue at the side of the beak as shown. Cut two #10 legs from orange paper and glue to the back of the body. Cut six #11 toes from orange paper. Glue three toes to the bottom of each leg as shown. With a black crayon or marker, draw on eyes.

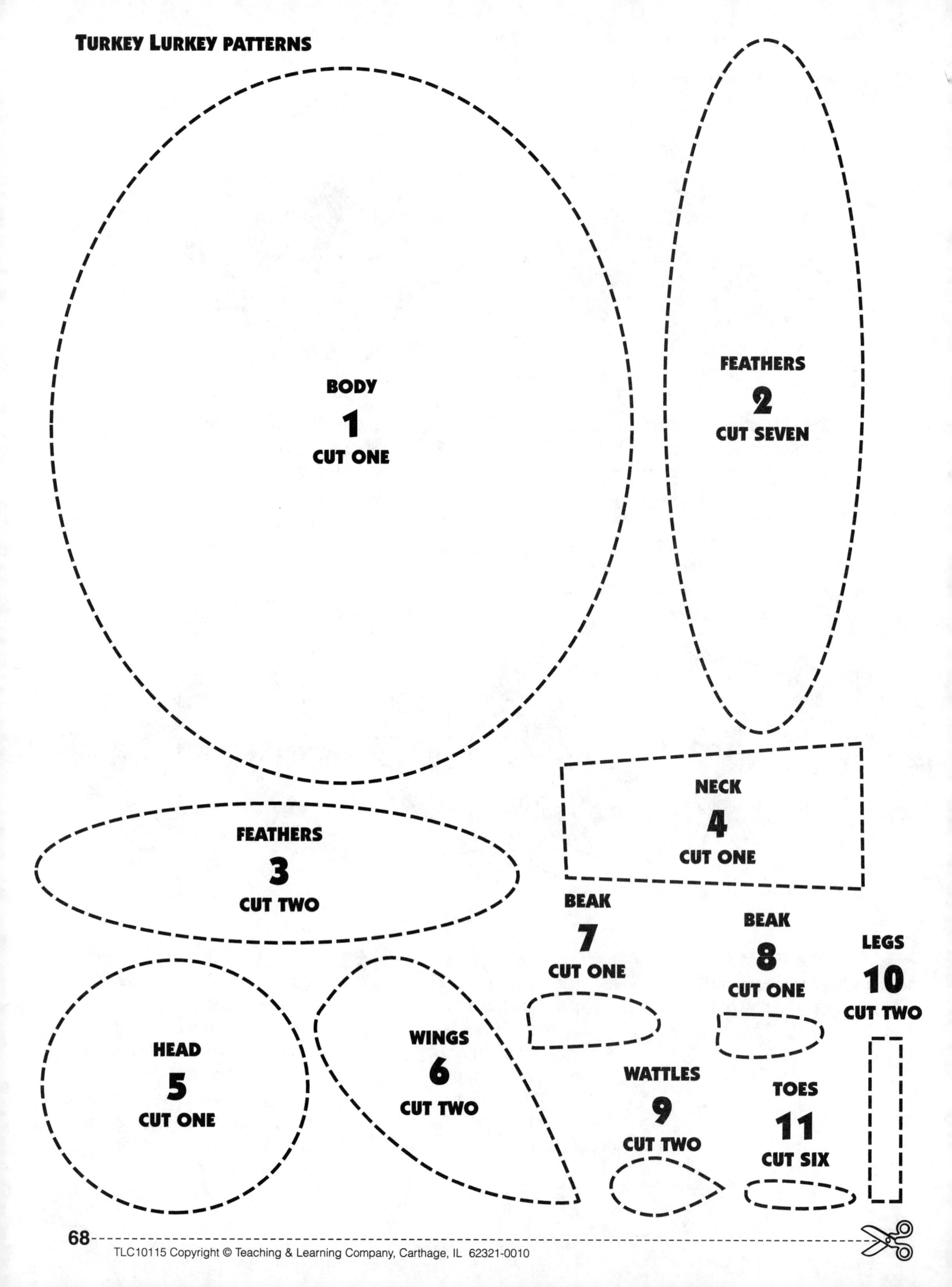
BODY
1
CUT ONE
FEATHERS
2
CUT SEVEN
FEATHERS
3
CUT TWO
NECK
4
CUT ONE
HEAD
5
CUT ONE
WINGS
6
CUT TWO
BEAK
7
CUT ONE
BEAK
8
CUT ONE
WATTLES
9
CUT TWO
LEGS
10
CUT TWO
TOES
11
CUT SIX

Little Red Riding Hood

Literature References

Little Red Riding Hood, by Brothers Grimm, illustrated by Trina Schart Hyman, New York: Holiday House, 1989.
Little Red Riding Hood, by Mirelle Levert, Buffalo, NY: Groundwood Books, 1996.
Little Red Riding Hood: Fay's Fairy Tales, by William Wegman, New York: Hyperion Books, 1993.
Little Red Riding Hood: Nursery Pop-Up Book, by Jonathan Langley, Hauppauge, NY: Barrons Juveniles, 1996.
Little Red Riding Hood, retold and illustrated by David McPhail, New York: Scholastic, 1995.

Note: Use the project on page 41 to represent the Wolf.

Materials: *black, blue, brown, gray, red and white paper; scissors; glue; black crayon or marker*
Optional Materials: *button*

RED RIDING HOOD

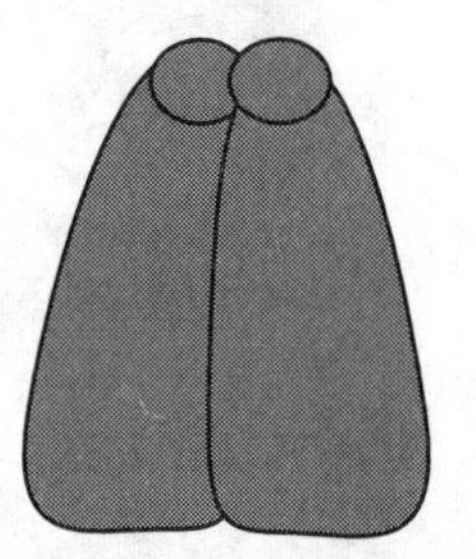

Cut two #1 capes from red paper. Cut two #2 collars from red paper. Glue one collar at the top of each cape as shown. Then glue the two capes together.

2 Cut one #3 hood from red paper. Cut one #4 inside hood from gray paper. Glue the inside hood to the red hood. Now glue the completed hood on top of the collars as illustrated.

3 Cut one #5 head from white paper and glue on top of the hood. Cut two #6 hairs from brown paper. Glue the hairs at the top of the head as illustrated.

Cut two #7 legs from blue paper. Glue the legs to the back of the cape as shown. Cut two #8 shoes from black paper. Glue one shoe to the bottom of each leg.

5 Cut two #9 eyes from white paper. Cut two #10 pupils from black paper. Glue the pupils on the eyes. Now glue the assembled eyes to the head as shown. With a black crayon or marker, draw on the mouth. Cut one #11 tongue from red paper and glue under the mouth as illustrated. Cut one #12 button from black paper and glue in place as shown.

6 Cut one #13 handle from brown paper. Cut one #14 inside basket from red paper. Cut one #15 basket from brown paper. Glue the inside basket over the handle. Now glue the basket to the bottom as illustrated. Cut two #16 hands from white paper and glue in place as shown.

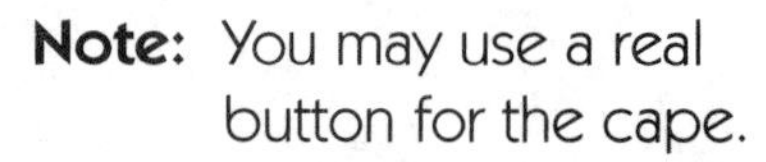

Note: You may use a real button for the cape.

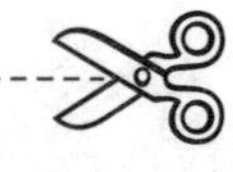

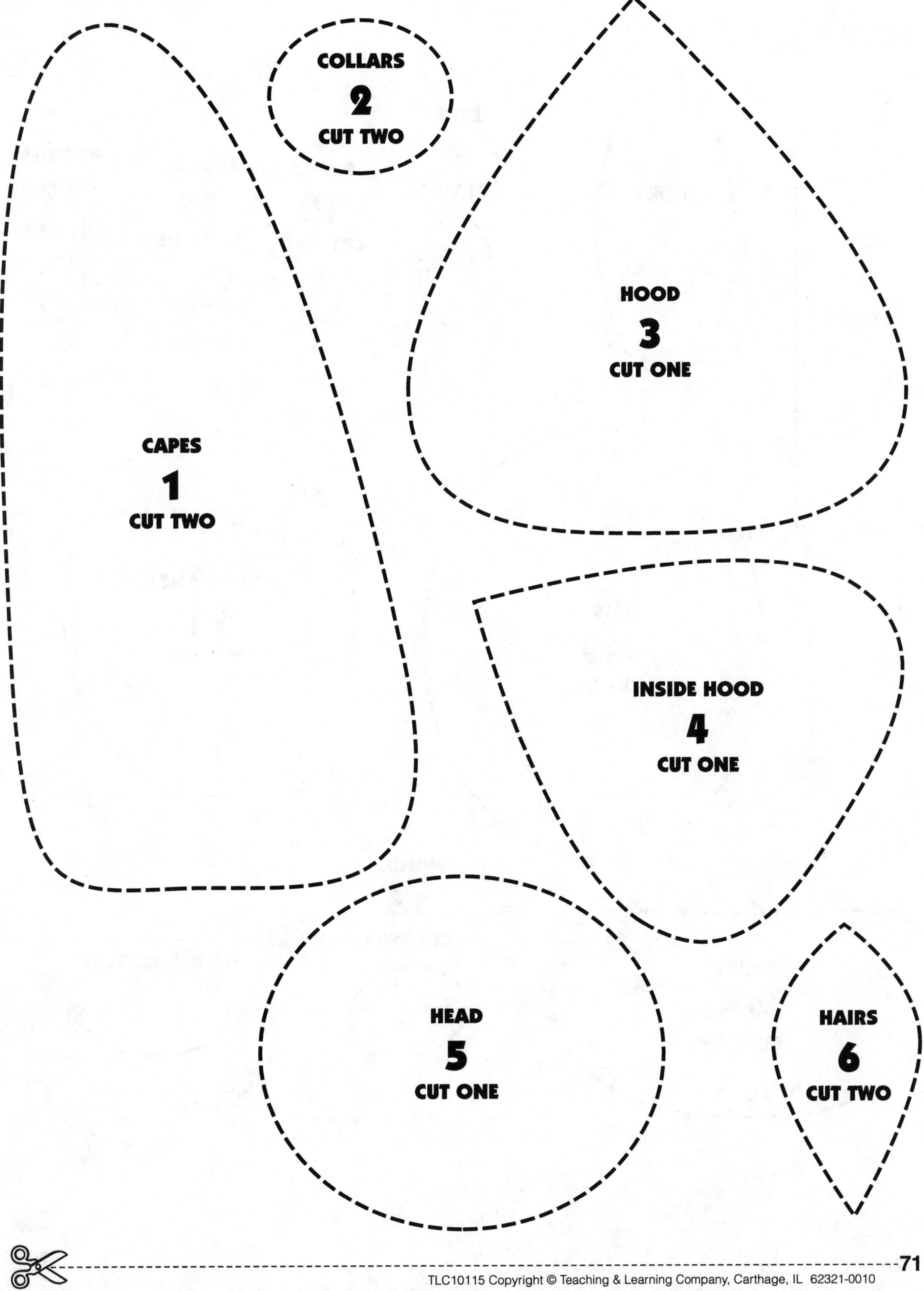
COLLARS
2
CUT TWO
HOOD
3
CUT ONE
CAPES
1
CUT TWO
INSIDE HOOD
4
CUT ONE
HEAD
5
CUT ONE
HAIRS
6
CUT TWO

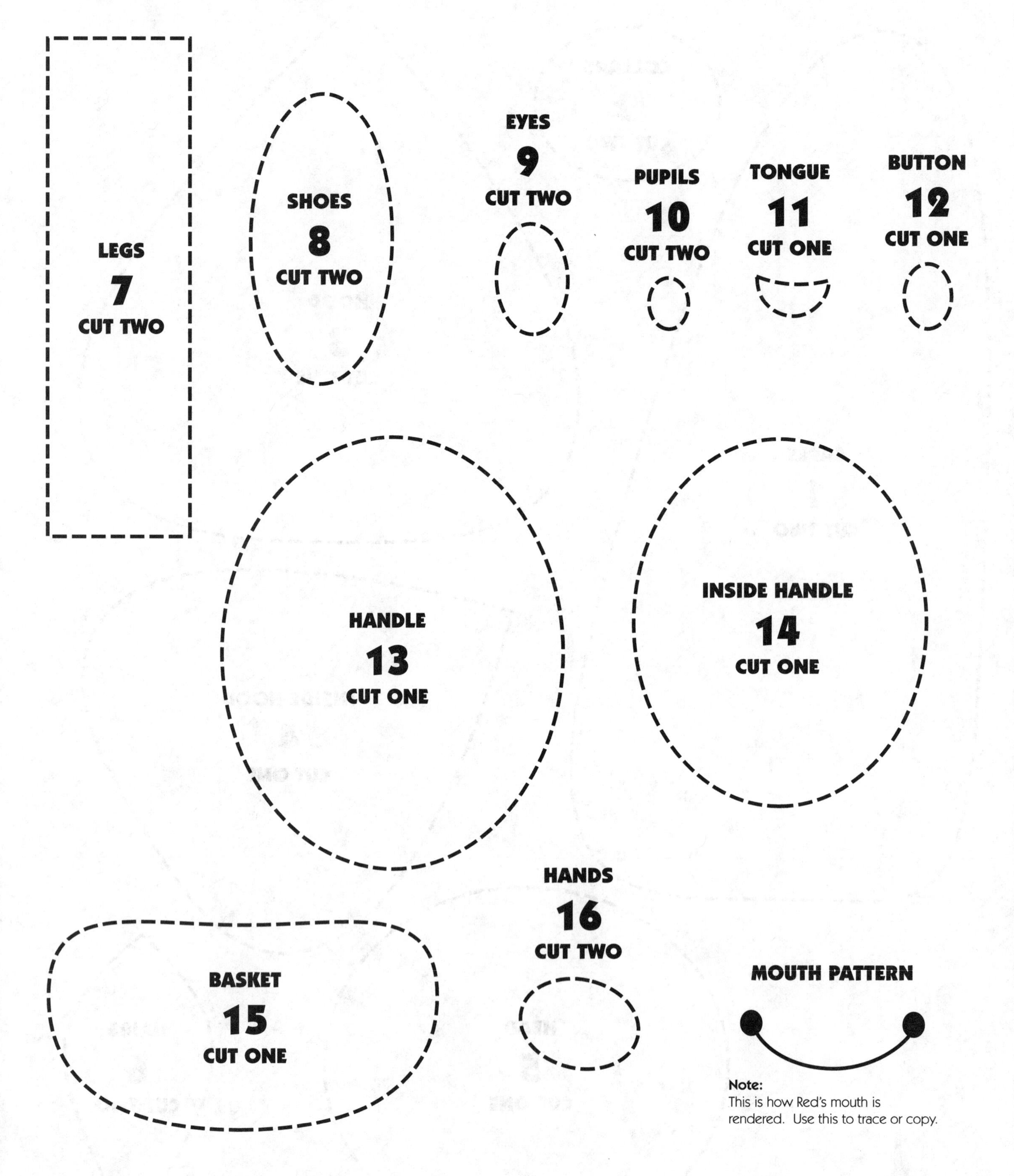

Note:
This is how Red's mouth is rendered. Use this to trace or copy.

Materials: *black, gray, flesh-colored, pink and white paper; scissors; glue; black crayon or marker; white crayon*

GRANDMA

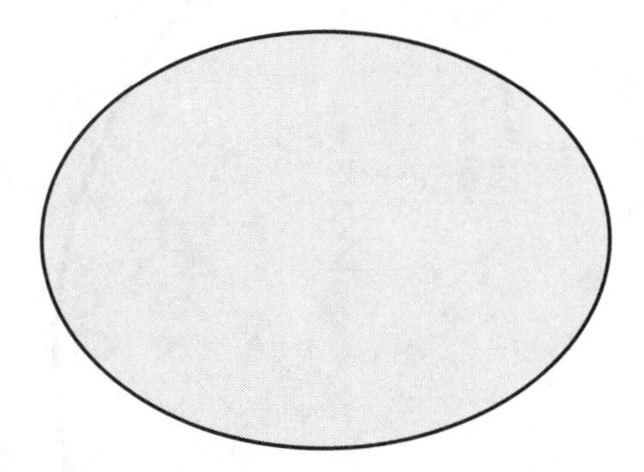

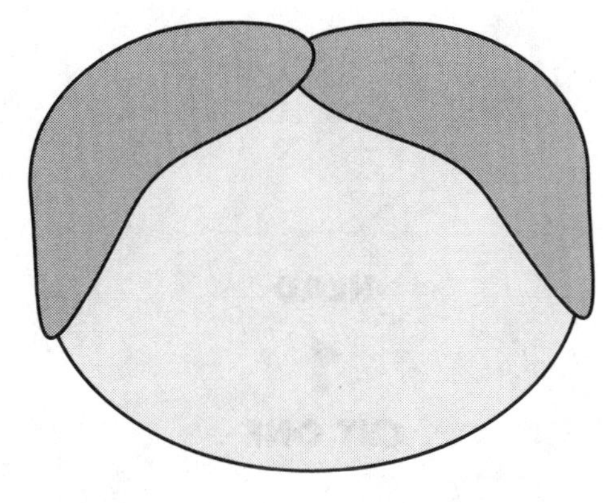

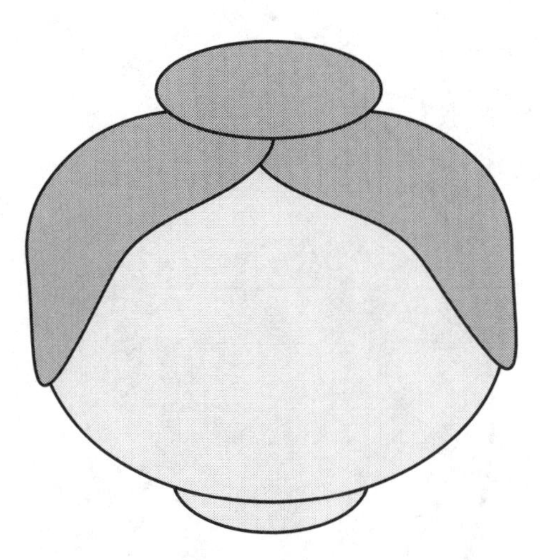

1. Cut one #1 head from flesh-colored paper.

2. Cut two #2 hairs from gray paper. Glue to the head as shown.

3. Cut two #3 bun/collar, one from flesh-colored paper and one from gray paper. Glue the flesh-colored piece at the bottom of the head to the back. Glue the gray piece to the top of the head as illustrated.

4. Cut two #4 eyes from black paper. Glue the eyes in place as illustrated. With a black crayon or marker, draw on glasses. Draw the pupils with a white crayon.

5. Cut one #5 lips from pink paper and glue on the head. With a black crayon or marker, draw on the eyebrows, eyelashes, nose, smile lines and line to divide the lips.

GRANDMA PATTERNS

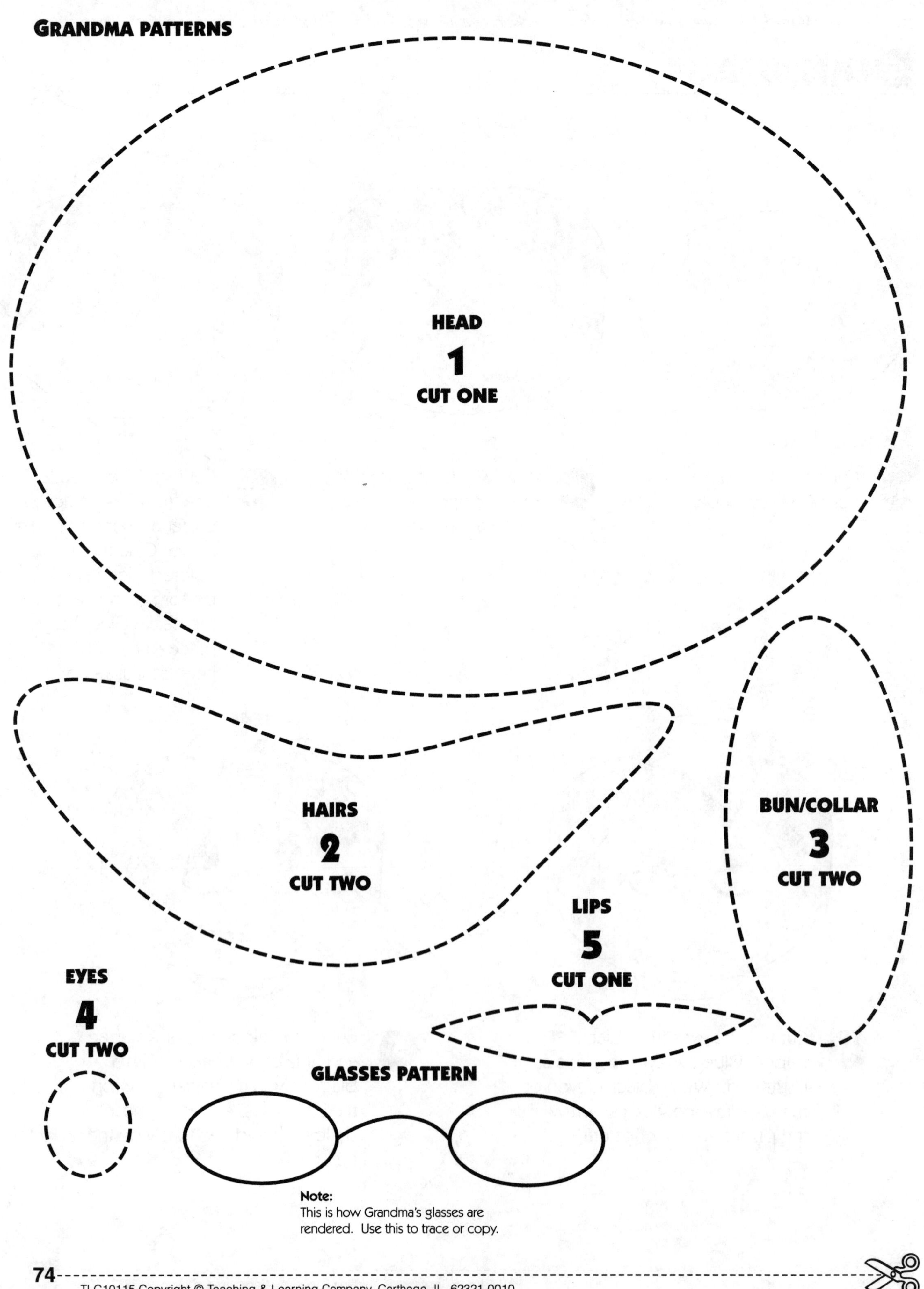

Note:
This is how Grandma's glasses are rendered. Use this to trace or copy.

Materials: *black, blue, brown, flesh-colored and white paper; scissors; glue; black crayon or marker; white crayon*

WOODSMAN

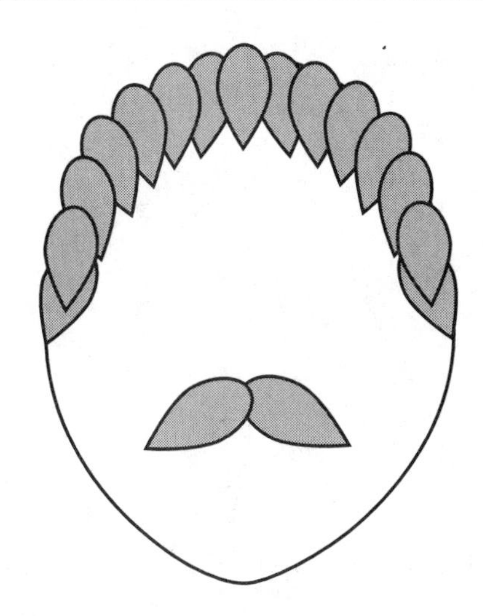

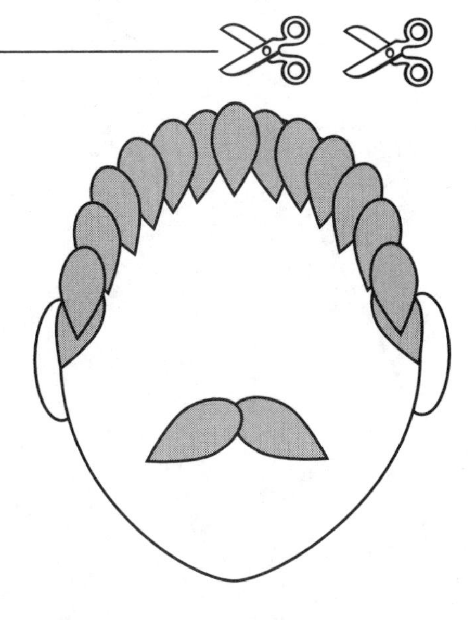

1 Cut one #1 head from flesh-colored paper.

Cut several #2 hairs from brown paper. Glue the pieces around the head as shown. Glue two pieces on the head for a mustache.

3 Cut two #3 ears from flesh-colored paper and glue to the back of the head.

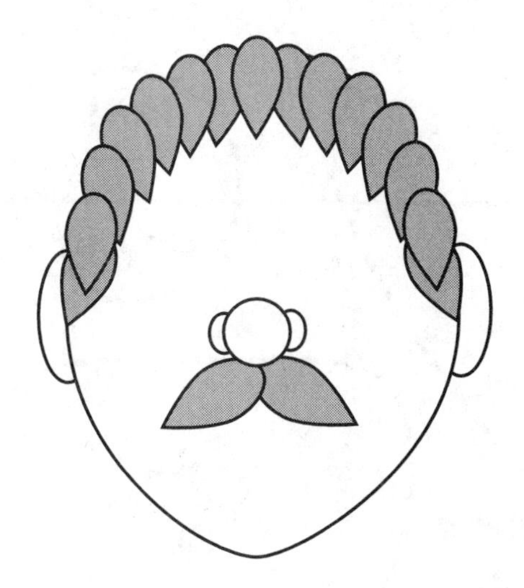

4 Cut one #4 nose and two #5 noses from flesh-colored paper. Glue the #5 noses to the back of the #4 nose. Now glue the assembled nose in place as shown.

5 Cut two #6 collars from blue paper and glue to the back of the head as illustrated. Cut two #7 eyes from white paper. Cut two #8 pupils from black paper. Glue the pupils on the eyes. Now glue the assembled eyes on the head as illustrated.

6 Cut one #9 beard from brown paper and glue at the bottom of the head. With a black crayon or marker, draw on eyebrows and mouth. With a white crayon, draw on the pupils as illustrated.

WOODSMAN PATTERNS

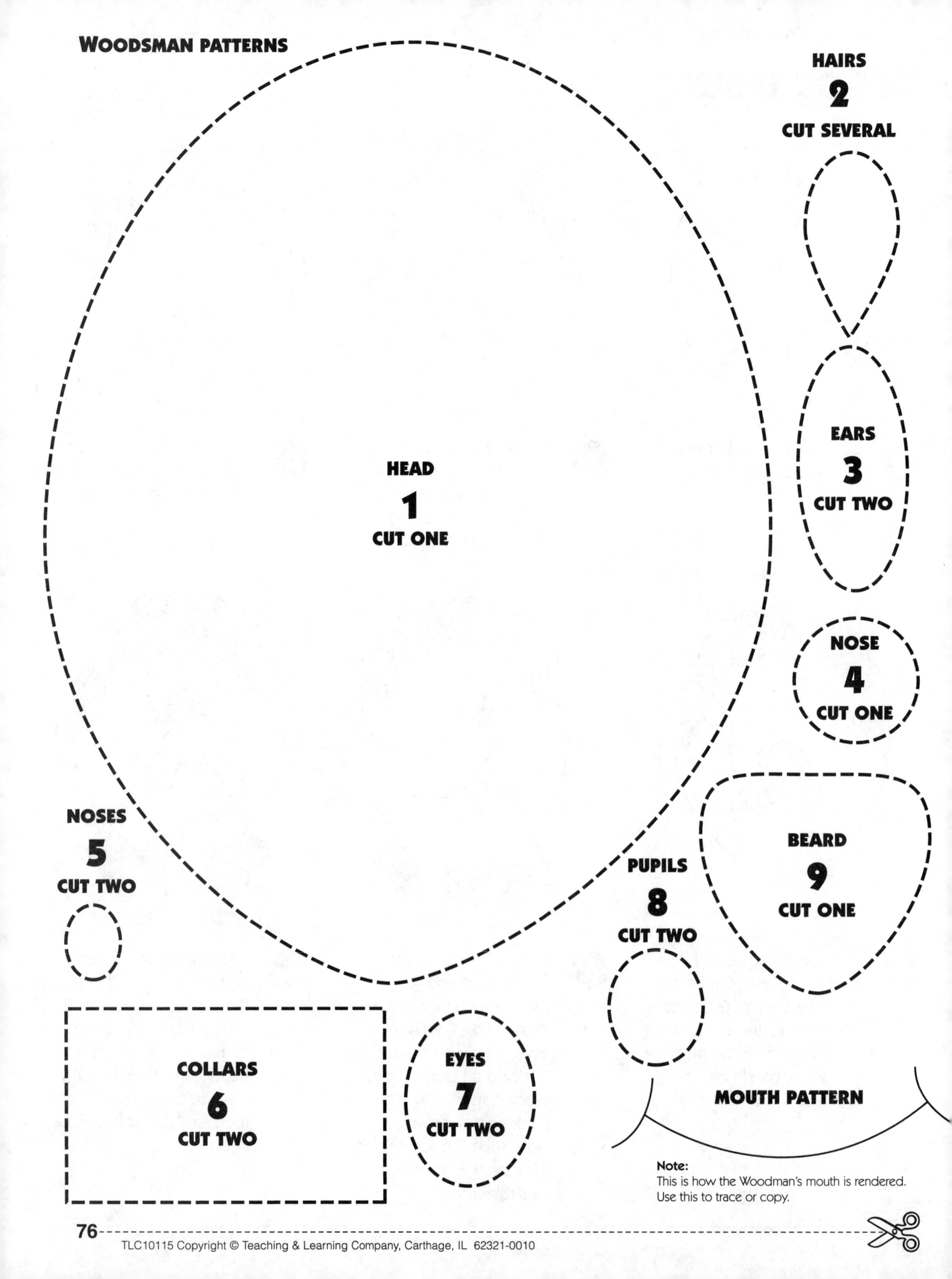

Note:
This is how the Woodman's mouth is rendered. Use this to trace or copy.

THE GINGERBREAD MAN

LITERATURE REFERENCES

The Gingerbread Man, by Pam Adams, Auburn, ME: Child's Play International, 1989.
The Gingerbread Man, by Eric A. Kimmel, illustrated by Megan Lloyd, New York: Holiday House, 1994.
The Gingerbread Man, illustrated by Karen Schmidt, New York: Scholastic, 1986.
The Gingerbread Man: An Old English Folktale, illustrated by John A. Rowe, New York: North-South Books, 1996.

Note: Use the project on page 61 to represent the Fox.

Materials: *black, brown or tan, red and a variety of colors of papers; scissors; glue; black crayon or marker*

Optional Materials: *buttons or raisins*

Gingerbread Man

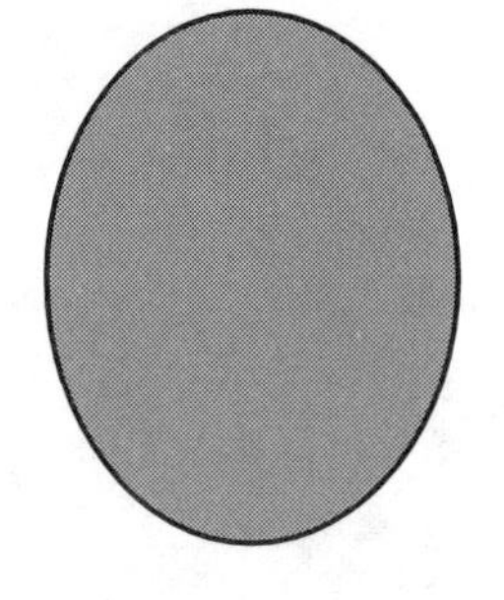

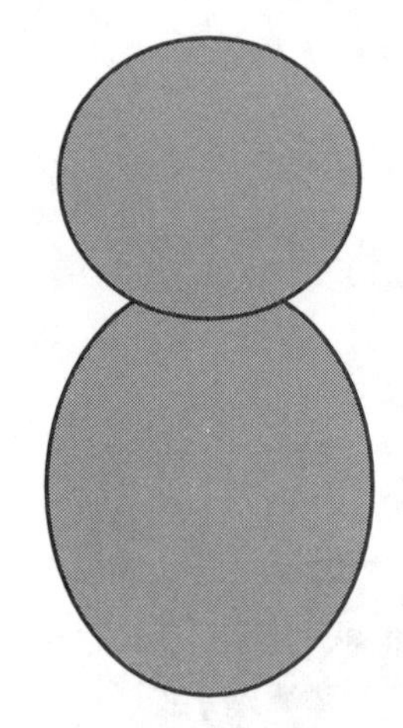

1. Cut one #1 body from brown or tan paper.

2. Cut one #2 head from brown or tan paper and glue to the top of the body.

3. Cut one #3 arms from brown or tan paper and glue to the back of the head and body as illustrated.

4. Cut two #4 legs from brown or tan paper. Glue the legs to the back of the body as shown.

5. Cut six #5 buttons/eyes/ nose pieces. Cut two from black paper (eyes). Cut one from red paper (nose), and cut three from whatever color you wish for buttons. Glue all the pieces in place as shown.

6. With a black crayon or marker, draw on the mouth.

Note: You may use real buttons or raisins on the body.

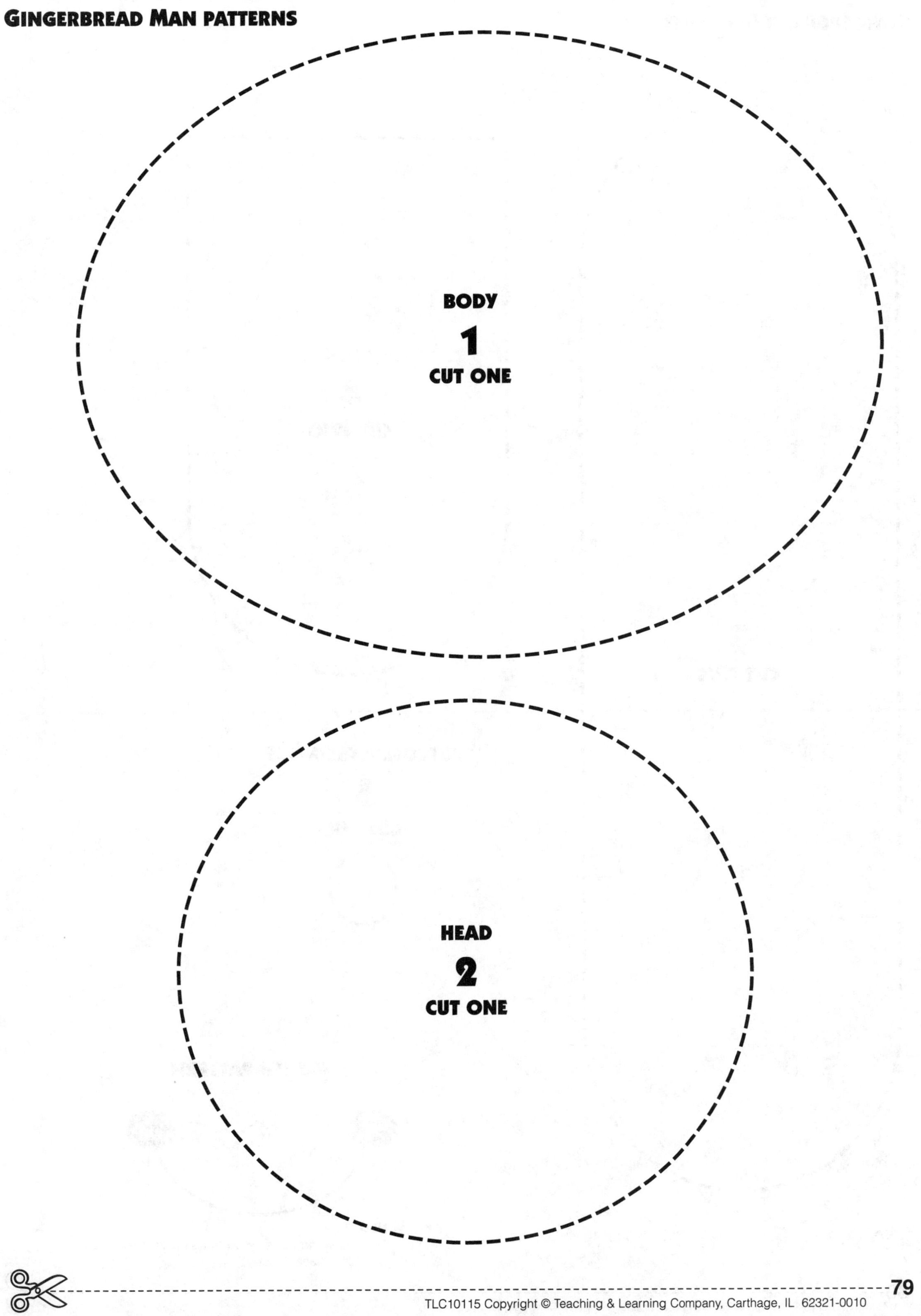
BODY
1
CUT ONE
HEAD
2
CUT ONE

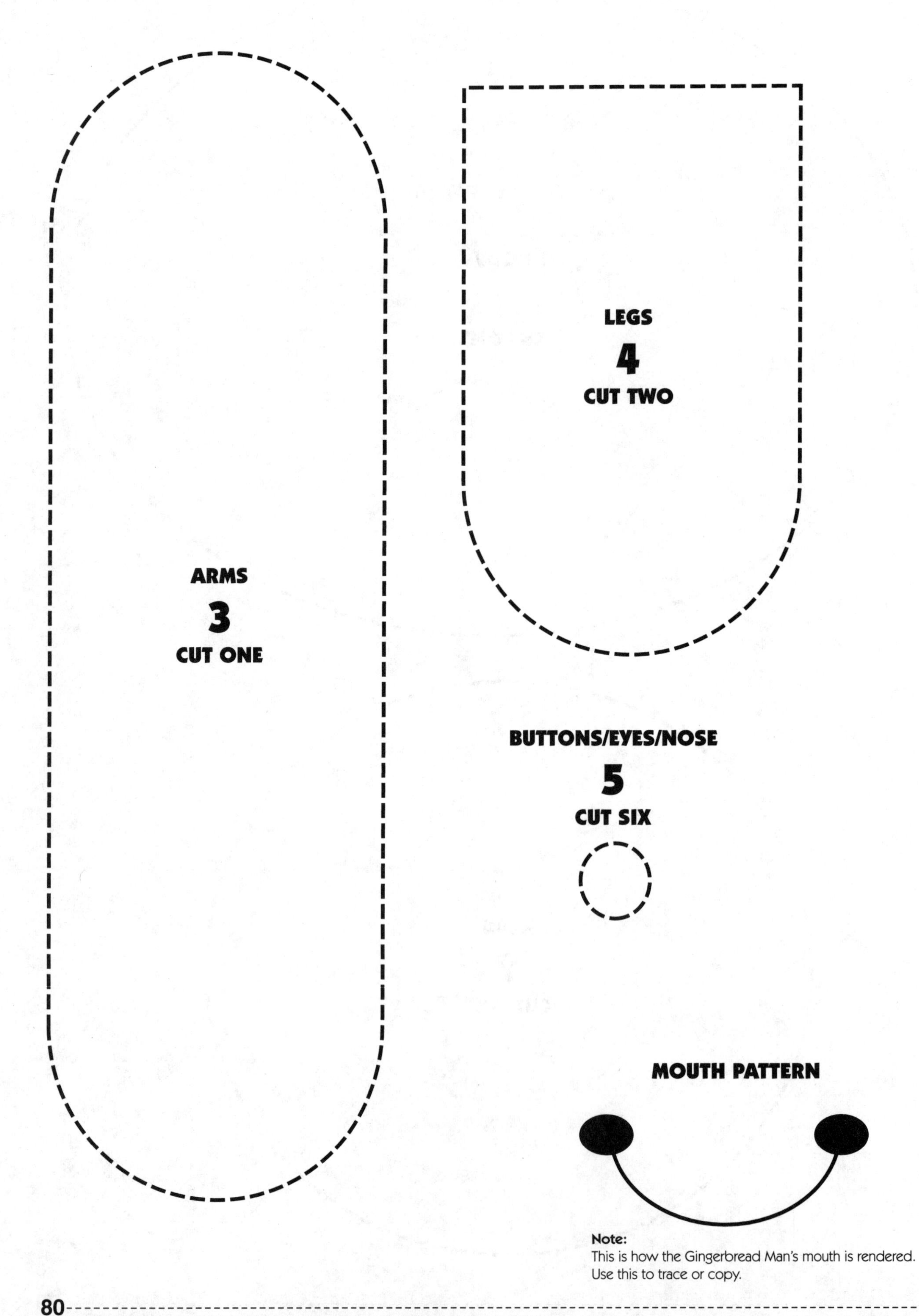

Note:
This is how the Gingerbread Man's mouth is rendered.
Use this to trace or copy.